MANDIE
AND THE
INVISIBLE
TROUBLEMAKER

Mandie Mysteries

MANDIE
AND THE
INVISIBLE
TROUBLEMAKER

Lois Gladys Leppard

BETHANY HOUSE PUBLISHERS
MINNEAPOLIS, MINNESOTA 55438

Mandie and the Invisible Troublemaker
Lois Gladys Leppard

All scripture quotations are taken from the
King James Version of the Bible.

Library of Congress Catalog Card Number 94–25134

ISBN 1–55661–510–8

Copyright © 1994
Lois Gladys Leppard
All Rights Reserved

Published by Bethany House Publishers
A Ministry of Bethany Fellowship, Inc.
11300 Hampshire Avenue South
Minneapolis, Minnesota 55438

Printed in the United States of America

Congratulations to
the winners of the Mandie's Fan Club
Mandie's Cookbook Contest.

Mary Elizabeth Warren
Atlanta, GA
Member #2187
For "Bessie's Lemon Pie" (p. 76)

and

Nathaniel Martin-Adkins
Hershey, PA
Member #652
For "Old-Time Divinity Candy" (p. 29)

And with love to all the other
hundreds of participants.

About the Author

LOIS GLADYS LEPPARD has been a Federal Civil Service employee in various countries around the world. She makes her home in South Carolina.

The stories of her own mother's childhood are the basis for many of the incidents incorporated in this series.

Contents

"Wait on the Lord: be of good courage, and he shall strengthen thine heart: wait, I say, on the Lord."

Psalm 27:14

Chapter 1 / Home Again

Mandie Shaw grabbed her bag and Snowball, her cat, and jumped down from the wagon as Uncle Ned brought it to a stop in the driveway. It had been a long journey through the North Carolina mountains from his house in Deep Creek, because travel in 1901 was slow.

"I really enjoyed my visit at your house, Uncle Ned," she told him.

The old Indian smiled down at her from the wagon seat and said, "Papoose come see again. Now I go."

"Don't forget to come back to see my mother and Uncle John," Mandie said.

"Soon." He began turning the wagon and said, "Papoose be good and think."

"I will," Mandie yelled back at him as she grasped Snowball while she swung her bag in the air and raced toward the front door, dragging Snowball along on his leash.

Dropping her bag and leaving Snowball in the front hall, she hurried to find her mother, Elizabeth, and Uncle John, who had married her mother after her father died. They were sitting in the parlor. Mandie was overcome with joy when she saw that her mother's cheeks were rosy and her eyes clear. Signs of the fever were finally gone!

"Amanda, darling, I'm so glad you're home," Elizabeth said as Mandie rushed to embrace her.

"I am, too, Mother. I love you. And, Uncle John, I love you, too," Mandie said as she turned to give him a big hug.

"And you know I love my little Blue Eyes," Uncle John said, patting her shoulder. "But where is Uncle Ned? He brought you home, didn't he?"

"Oh yes, he asked me to tell y'all he had other places to go and he'd see y'all later," Mandie explained.

"Just like Uncle Ned," Uncle John said, looking at Elizabeth. "He knew this would be a special time for just us, having Amanda back home."

Mandie plopped down on the footstool in front of her mother and asked, "Now that I'm back home, couldn't I just stay home, Mother? Grandmother sent me a letter with Uncle Ned when he went to Asheville on business. She said my school may be sold. So couldn't I just stay home now?"

"No, I'm sorry, dear, but you must return to school," Elizabeth answered. "The Heathwoods haven't even found a prospective buyer for the school yet—and they may never find one. So back to the Misses Heathwood's School for you."

"I hope they won't ever be able to sell the school," Mandie said with a slight smile.

Elizabeth looked at her and asked, "Do you

mean you're hoping the school won't change hands? And last year, you didn't want to go there."

Mandie frowned as she replied, "Well, you see, Celia and I might not end up together in another school if we have to leave that one. Besides, the new owners might just fire Aunt Phoebe and Uncle Cal because they're getting old."

Elizabeth reached to smooth Mandie's blond hair as Mandie removed her bonnet and dangled it by the strings. "I'm sure Celia's mother and I could agree on a school for you two if you have to leave the Heathwoods'. And I don't imagine that school could run without Aunt Phoebe and Uncle Cal. Why, they've been there so long, they're permanent fixtures," her mother said.

"I hope you're right," Mandie said.

At that moment, Liza, the young Negro maid, appeared in the doorway. She became excited when she saw Mandie. "Lawsy mercy, Missy 'Manda, I sho' is glad you's back," she said. "Been too quiet heah wid you gone."

Mandie ran to embrace the girl and said, "I'm glad to be back, Liza. But you know I have to get ready to go back to school in Asheville in a few days."

"I knows, Missy 'Manda. So do Aunt Lou. You gotta see whut Aunt Lou done. She been sewin' night and day since you went to visit dat Injun man. She made all kinda fancy dresses fo' you to take to dat school," Liza said, dancing happily around as she talked.

Mandie gasped and said, "She made me new dresses? But I've got so many clothes now that I'll never be able to wear them out."

"Dear," said Elizabeth from across the room,

"of course you'll never be able to wear out all your clothes for the simple reason that you are outgrowing them. But there are plenty of girls we can find who need them."

Mandie looked at her mother, then back at Liza. "Am I outgrowing my clothes? But, Mother, I haven't grown a fraction of an inch in the last year."

Elizabeth laughed and replied, "You'll be surprised when you put on some of the dresses that were made for you a year ago to take to school."

Mandie glanced down at the blue gingham dress she was wearing. She flipped her skirt around. "I don't believe this one is any smaller on me." Then looking at Liza, she asked, "Where is Aunt Lou? I've just got to see how big she's making these new clothes."

"She be in de sewin' room upstairs, Missy 'Manda. And she know you home. Dat white cat, Snowball, he done been round lettin' ev'ybody know you's back," Liza said.

Mandie glanced at her mother. Now that she was home, she didn't want to leave her mother for a single moment. She had almost lost her when the fever struck.

"Go ahead, dear. Aunt Lou may need to do some fitting," Elizabeth told her.

"I won't be gone long," Mandie promised. She followed Liza out into the hallway and picked up her bag.

Mandie found Aunt Lou laying out material on a worktable in the sewing room and rushed to embrace the old Negro woman. "I love you, Aunt Lou. I've missed you," Mandie told her as she threw her arms around the woman's large waist.

"I've missed you too, my chile," Aunt Lou replied, squeezing Mandie against her, then holding her back to look down into Mandie's face. "But we got work to do. We'se gwine make you de bes' dressed young lady at dat school in Asheville." She pointed around the room at several dresses, hanging from whatever their hangers would catch on.

"Oh, Aunt Lou! They're all so beautiful!" Mandie cried, rushing from one to another. She stopped suddenly to ask, "But, Aunt Lou, how did you know what size to make these dresses when I wasn't here to try them on?"

Aunt Lou reached for Mandie's hand and pulled her up beside her. "Heah," the old woman said as she marked Mandie's height against her own shoulder. "You done growed. Last time I made dresses you could walk under my arm. Now you reach my shoulder. You see?"

Mandie gasped in surprise. "Why, I didn't realize I had grown any at all. Mother said I had, but I didn't really believe her." She smiled and looked up. "Pretty soon I'll be as tall as you are, Aunt Lou."

"Now I doubts dat, my chile. You done turned thirteen year old, and most times when people reach dat age they done growed all they gwine grow." Aunt Lou turned back to the table where she had been cutting out a dress and said, "Now git along wid you. I got one mo' dress heah to make 'fo' you goes back to school—and dat ain't long off."

Mandie ran her hand across the smooth, pink silk material as Aunt Lou laid a pattern on it. "Oh, Aunt Lou, it's so soft and silky. Thank you for making me such beautiful clothes," she said. She picked up her bag, which she had left by the doorway, and added, "I have to take this to my room and then I'll go back downstairs. See you later." She threw the old woman a kiss as she left the room.

After Mandie had left the bag in her room, she raced down the stairs, almost colliding with Jason Bond, Uncle John's caretaker, at the foot of the steps.

"Slow down there!" the gray-haired man told her with a big smile as he caught her by the arm to keep her from falling. "I want to take you back to school in one piece," he laughed.

Mandie looked up at him, smiled, and said, "I'm sorry, Mr. Jason. Are you going to take me back to school?"

"That's what Mr. Shaw said. He doesn't want to let your mother out of his sight, and she's not well enough to travel," Mr. Bond explained.

"I'm glad Uncle John is taking such good care of my mother," Mandie said. "And I'm glad you're going to Asheville with me." She paused and sniffed the air. "M-m-m-m! I smell something good cooking. I'll just slip into the kitchen and see what Jenny's doing."

Mr. Bond smiled at her and continued on down the corridor. Mandie softly pushed open the door to the kitchen and looked inside. Jenny, the Negro cook, was bending over the oven door of the big iron cookstove.

"A cake!" Mandie cried.

"Sh-h-h-h! Don't shake de floor or it won't be no cake. It'll fall," Jenny told her.

Mandie caught her breath and stood perfectly still. "I'm sorry, Jenny," she said. "I know it'll make the cake go flat if I shake the floor. It smelled so good I had to see what you were doing."

Jenny pulled the broomstraw out of one of the layers of cake in the oven and stood up to look at the straw. "It be done anyhow," she said. She picked up two heavy towels to use as potholders and took the pans from the oven.

Mandie watched and counted, "Four layers! Oh, Jenny, that's going to be a big cake!"

Jenny closed the oven door and straightened up. She held out her arms and Mandie ran to her embrace.

"It be special, it do," Jenny said. "You done got home and yo' mama done got bettuh. We celebrate wid a big four-layer cake all covered wid chocolate icin' 'cause it gwine be a while 'fo' Missy gits back home agin from dat school."

"Oh, thank you, Jenny!" Mandie exclaimed with a big smile. "I sure won't be late for supper."

The back door opened, and Abraham, Jenny's husband, pushed through, his arms loaded with wood for the cookstove. He hurried to the bin nearby to stack it.

"Abraham! I'm back home," Mandie said, excitedly rushing to squeeze the black man's big hand as he straightened up.

Abraham squeezed Mandie's hand and said, "I see you is. We done be missin' you, Missy 'Manda."

"But I won't be here long. I have to go back to that school in Asheville, and it'll be a long time before I can get a holiday to come home," Mandie told him.

Abraham frowned and looked at Mandie seriously as he told her, "But, Missy 'Manda, don't you fuss 'bout dat. Be thankful you kin git eddicated."

Mandie quickly became solemn as she replied, "I am thankful, Abraham. I just hate going off and leaving my mother so long when I only found her last year."

"Dat bad yo' mama and papa got separated when you born, but you ought not dwell on bad things," Jenny spoke up. "Think how good things be now."

"You are both right. I can't change the past. I can only hope to help make the future brighter," Mandie said. "And right now I've got to go back to see my mother. See y'all at suppertime."

Mandie hurried back to the parlor and sat down next to her mother just as Liza came hurrying in to say, "Missy Polly, she be at de do'."

Polly Cornwallis was Mandie's next-door neighbor. Mandie tried to be friends with the girl, but sometimes Polly was hard to be nice to. Mandie wondered what Polly wanted now.

Before anyone could reply to Liza, Polly appeared behind her in the hallway and stepped through the doorway. "I'm glad you're home, Mandie. I just wanted to talk to you for a few minutes," Polly said, glancing at Elizabeth and John Shaw.

"Go ahead, dear," Elizabeth urged Mandie, who was reluctant to talk to the girl. "We'll see you at suppertime. That's not long off."

"All right, Mother," said Mandie. She stood up and joined Polly in the doorway and said, "Come on, let's sit on the front porch."

The two girls went to the veranda and sat in the swing, and Mandie pushed it back and forth with her foot.

Polly put both her feet on the floor and said, "Be still a minute, Mandie. I have some exciting news." She turned to face Mandie. Her eyes, black as chinquapins, sparkled with excitement.

"What?" Mandie asked, not too interested.

"I am going to your school this year," Polly began with a big smile.

Mandie was immediately interested. Polly had been going to a very expensive girls' school in another city. "Why?" she asked.

Polly frowned and asked, "Why? You don't want me to go to school with you?"

"Oh, Polly, I didn't say that," Mandie replied. "Why are you not going back to the school you've been attending?"

"Well, give me a chance to explain," Polly said. "My mother has decided Asheville is much nearer home. Therefore, I could come home more often. And not only that, but Miss Prudence Heathwood has cut her prices. They are putting the school up for sale. Therefore, they are trying to get more girls to go there so it will look good to prospective buyers."

Mandie sighed and said, "I know. My grandmother wrote me that they were trying to sell the school. But my mother says they may never be able to. I hope they keep it until I finish there. I have three more years to go, I suppose."

"And I will probably stay there until I finish, too," Polly added. She suddenly stood up and said, "I have to go home now. I just couldn't wait to tell you that I'll be going to school with you."

Mandie stood up and asked, "Are you going with me when I go back to school?"

"Oh no, my mother has to take me, but I'll be seeing you there," Polly said. "Maybe we'll even share a room. That would be fun."

Mandie groaned inwardly. Sharing a room with Polly would never work out. Besides, Mandie had taken it for granted that she and Celia would be able to share the same room they had the previous school year. She'd just have to get back to school before Polly and make sure she and Celia ended up together.

"When are you leaving?" Mandie asked as Polly walked down the steps of the porch. "I'll be going back to school next Monday."

"My mother and I have already been there to get me registered," Polly said. "Miss Prudence gave me permission to be a day late checking in. We're having some important company at our house, and they won't be leaving until the day you leave for school. So I'll be coming along the next day."

Polly turned and strolled slowly down the walkway and into the side yard. "See you then," she called before she hurried on through the trees toward her house next door.

Mandie sighed and went back inside the house. She glanced into the parlor and found it was empty. When she looked at the big grandfather clock standing in the hallway, she realized she'd have to hurry to bathe and change clothes in time for supper.

"Thank goodness I'll be getting to school a day ahead of Polly so I can be sure Celia and I get our old room back," Mandie mumbled to herself as she flipped through the dresses hanging in her chifferobe. She quickly pulled down a pink, flowered cotton dress and spread it across her blue-covered bed.

Before long, Mandie was ready to go downstairs to supper. She saw that her mother and Uncle John were waiting for her in the parlor. When Jason Bond came in right behind her, they all went into the dining room and seated themselves at the table.

"Mother, did you know Polly is going to my school this year?" Mandie asked as Liza started bringing in the food.

"Yes, dear. In fact, I told her mother it would be all right for you to wait until Tuesday to go back to school so Polly could go along with you and Mr. Bond. That way her mother wouldn't have to make the trip," Elizabeth explained.

Mandie gasped and said, "But, Mother, I . . . I . . . don't want to wait till Tuesday. I want to go Monday."

Elizabeth looked at her in surprise and said, "I thought maybe you'd like an extra day at home before you leave."

"Oh no, Mother," Mandie began—and then she realized her mother might think she was in a hurry to leave home again. "I mean, Mother, I . . . well, to be honest, I just want to get to school *before* Polly does. She said we could maybe share a room. But I don't want to share a room with her. I want to get the same room with Celia again this year."

Elizabeth smiled and said, "All right, dear. That's fine. I understand." She turned to Mr. Bond and said, "Then you will be leaving Monday instead of Tuesday."

"Yes, ma'am," Mr. Bond said with a big grin. Mandie knew he understood.

"Thank you, Mother," Mandie said. And with a big smile she added, "It's not that I want to leave you a day earlier than I have to. I just don't want to be stuck with Polly. We don't . . . understand each other too well sometimes."

"That's fine, dear," Elizabeth said as she began passing the food. "I'm sure Polly's mother won't mind. In fact, I believe some of the relatives who are coming to visit them will be going back through Asheville, and Polly could just go with them."

Suddenly the swinging door to the hallway was pushed open and Joe Woodard appeared. "Hello," he said, looking around the room. "My father had to come to see some patients here in Franklin, so I came with him."

Aunt Lou came in behind him and said, "I lets him in, Miz 'Liz'beth." She turned to Joe and showed him to an empty chair at the table next to Mandie. "Jes' you sits down right dere and I gits 'nuther plate."

Joe did as he was told, and everyone began talking at once while Aunt Lou went back to get dishes and silverware for him.

"I'm glad you were able to come with your father, Joe," Elizabeth said as she passed the biscuits. "Help yourself now."

"Thank you, ma'am," Joe replied as he took a biscuit and accepted the bowl of mashed potatoes from Mandie. "My father will be back tonight after he makes his rounds."

"Then you're going to be able to stay a few days?" Mandie asked excitedly.

"That is, if your mother asks us," Joe said with a laugh.

"Joe, you know you don't have to wait to be asked," Elizabeth told him. "You and your father are always welcome here—and your mother too, whenever she can make it."

"Thank you, ma'am," Joe said.

"Oh, Joe, I'm glad you came," Mandie said. "You'll never believe what's happened."

Joe quickly looked at her, but Elizabeth stopped the conversation. "I think we'd better eat first, then you and Joe can talk," she told Mandie.

"Yes, ma'am," Mandie said with a disappointed sigh. She looked at Joe and smiled. "Let's hurry and get through."

"It won't be hard for me to hurry. I'm starved, and all this food smells so good!" Joe exclaimed as he accepted the bowls and platters passed around the table toward him.

"It sure does," Mandie agreed. She glanced at her mother's plate. She seemed to be eating better now. When Mandie had gone to visit Uncle Ned, her mother was just recovering from the fever. Now she seemed almost completely well.

Uncle John noticed Mandie observing her mother and said, "Nothing to worry about now, Amanda. You see, your mother is getting back to her old self."

Mandie remembered the relatives who had come to visit during Elizabeth's illness. "Do you think the kinpeople will come to visit again?" she asked.

"They promised they would," Uncle John replied. He grinned big and added, "They all seemed to be taken with you. I wonder why?"

Before Mandie could reply, Joe laughed and said, "Yes, I wonder why?"

"Oh, let's just finish our supper so we can go talk," Mandie said with a sigh. "There is something I want to discuss with you."

"Not another mystery, I hope," Joe said. He smiled as he cut the piece of ham on his plate and watched Mandie out of the corner of his eye.

"Of course not," Mandie said. "It's more important than a mystery." She gave Joe a solemn look, and the smile immediately faded from his face.

Mandie was anxious to discuss her visit to Uncle Ned's house with Joe, and she also wanted to tell him about Polly. She could hardly wait to get away from the supper table.

But then Jenny brought in the huge chocolate-covered cake, and Mandie's attention became focused entirely on it. Joe devoured two pieces before everyone left the table. Afterward, Mandie quickly led him out onto the front porch to talk.

Chapter 2 / Trouble Begins

Mandie led the way and she and Joe plopped down in the swing on the front porch.

"Well?" Joe questioned as he turned to look at her.

"Well, it's like this," Mandie began with a deep frown. "Polly Cornwallis is going to my school this year and—"

"Mandie, it's not *your* school. You don't own it," Joe teased.

"You just gave me an idea. Maybe I could get Uncle John to buy it. It's for sale, you know," Mandie said thoughtfully.

"I can't imagine your uncle John buying a girls' school, but what is it that you're upset about?" Joe asked.

"As I said, Polly is going to my school and, not only that, she wants to share a room with me, which I absolutely refuse to do," Mandie said firmly.

"There's no rule that says you have to, is there?" Joe asked.

"No, but my mother told her mother that I would even wait a day to return to school so Polly could go with me and Mr. Jason," Mandie explained. "Anyhow, I told my mother I didn't want to share a room or wait for Polly, that I wanted to get back on time because I hope Celia and I will be able to share a room again this year."

"I don't see any problem, then," Joe said, smiling. "Remember, if Miss Prudence gives you any trouble about sharing a room with Celia, just ask your grandmother to speak to her."

"That's another good idea," Mandie said. "My grandmother does have a lot of influence with Miss Prudence. I'm glad she lives near the school."

"Tell me what you did at Uncle Ned's house," Joe said. "Did anything exciting happen?"

"I'll say exciting things happened," Mandie said with a big grin. "But we got it all worked out. Two strange men were digging all over the mountain, and Sallie got kidnapped, then Uncle Dimar disappeared. Oh, I wish you could have been there." Mandie went into detail about her visit to Uncle Ned's house, and Joe listened to every word.

"A lot of things sure did happen in a short time," Joe said with a sigh.

"Yes," Mandie agreed. "And I suppose things will seem dull at school."

Joe cleared his throat, ran his long fingers through his unruly brown hair, then said with a big grin, "I'll come and liven things up if you'd like."

"You will?" Mandie asked quickly. "But how?"

"I don't know. My father has to go to Asheville soon for a few days, and he has promised I can go with him," Joe explained, still smiling.

"Oh, that would be great!" Mandie exclaimed. Then she looked at Joe and asked, "But how are you going to do that? You're supposed to go to school, you know."

"Don't forget we have harvest break back in the country. My father and I will come then because we don't have to harvest our crops. My father has tenant farms looking after everything and—"

"Oh, Joe, I'm so glad you're coming to Asheville," Mandie interrupted. "We can have a great time." Her tone suddenly changed, and she asked, "Have you been up the mountain lately?"

Joe reached for her hand and held it tightly. "Yes, I was going to tell you. I took flowers up to your father's grave the last thing before we left home," he said softly. "And everything looked fine."

Mandie put her other hand on top of his and replied, "Thanks, Joe. I hope I can go up there sometime soon. It's been a long time, even though it was only April of last year that I lost my father."

"I went up the road near your father's house, but I didn't see anyone around there—not your stepmother, her husband, or her daughter. It seemed empty. There weren't any chickens in the yard, but I couldn't go close enough to be sure. I don't believe there was a single cow or a horse around either," he explained.

Mandie withdrew her hands, straightened up to look at Joe, and asked, "Do you suppose those people have moved out of my father's house?"

"I'm not sure but I'll find out for you when I go home," Joe promised.

"Someday I'm going to get my father's house

back," Mandie said wistfully.

"You sure are," Joe promised with a smile. "Because I am going to get it back for you when we grow up, so you will have to keep your promise and marry me."

"We'll see," Mandie said. She looked down the long walkway and saw Dr. Woodard stop his buggy, step down and open the gate, then drive on into the yard.

"Your father is here."

"So I see," Joe said as he stood up. "I'll take the horse for him." He hurried down to meet his father.

Mandie watched as Dr. Woodard turned the buggy and horse over to Joe and came on over to the front porch. Joe drove the vehicle around to the backyard.

"And how is Miss Amanda?" Dr. Woodard said as he came up the steps. He removed his wide-brimmed hat and wiped his forehead with a handkerchief. "It's certainly warm for this time of the year."

"Yes, it is, Dr. Woodard. Come on in. Aunt Lou has saved supper for you," Mandie said as she rose, and he followed her through the front door.

Aunt Lou had not only saved supper for Dr. Woodard, but the adults were still sitting around the dining room table drinking coffee. Aunt Lou seated Dr. Woodard, and Mandie and Joe sat down next to him.

Mandie had a reason for sitting at the table again. As soon as she could get a word in, she said, "I have a great idea, Uncle John. Why don't you just buy my school from Miss Prudence and Miss Hope? I'm sure it wouldn't cost a whole lot." She smiled at him as he turned to look at her.

"Oh now, Amanda," Uncle John said as every-one at the table became silent. "I don't think I would want to engage in the business of a young ladies' school. This young lady right here named Amanda is quite a handful for me." He laughed.

Mandie frowned and tapped her foot under the table as she impatiently replied, "Uncle John, I'm serious. You could at least buy it and keep it until I finish, and then you could sell it." She wanted to make sure she sounded serious.

"Amanda," Uncle John said, still smiling. "Most of the time I know I let you have your way, but this time it's just not feasible for me to buy a school over in Asheville." He paused, then continued, "Say, why don't you ask your grandmother to buy it? Mrs. Taft lives in Asheville and just might be interested."

"Do you think so?" Mandie asked, excited about this new possibility.

"Yes, I truly think so," her uncle said.

Mandie looked at her mother. Elizabeth smiled and said, "You know, my mother owns so many other things that it probably wouldn't be any trouble for her to take on a girls' school, too. We should have thought of this before."

"De Lawd haf mercy on dat po' grandma," Liza muttered from where she stood by the sideboard.

"I agree," Joe remarked with a big grin. "Be-cause knowing Mandie, she won't stop until she gets what she wants."

Mandie frowned as she looked at him and said, "That's not so, Joe Woodard. I only plan to *talk* to my grandmother about buying my school. I can't *make* her buy it."

"Now, Amanda, you know those blue eyes can melt your grandmother's heart just like they do mine," Uncle John teased.

"But not mine," Elizabeth said. "Now, I think we've heard enough of this for the time being."

"Yes, Mother. I'll let y'all know what my grandmother has to say after I see her," Mandie promised.

Mandie and Joe left the table to go outside for a walk in the yard, which Mandie decided was a big mistake when she saw Polly Cornwallis rushing over to follow them around. Mandie knew Polly was only doing this to get a chance to talk to Joe.

After the three had walked together for a short distance, Mandie decided to be blunt with Polly about her plans for going to school. She stopped and looked at the dark-haired girl, saying, "I am not going to wait until Tuesday to go back to school, Polly. I am leaving Monday just like I'm supposed to. My mother says your relatives will be able to take you back to Asheville with them on Tuesday."

Polly quickly looked at Mandie and said, "That's all right. I don't mind going with my relatives." She turned to Joe and asked, "How long are *you* staying with the Shaws? Will you still be here on Monday?"

Mandie instantly understood why Polly wanted her to go to Asheville on Monday. Polly was hoping to have time alone with Joe after Mandie left.

"I don't know right now," Joe said. "My father hasn't told me yet. But I do know that as soon as he finishes his calls we will go home."

Mandie secretly hoped Dr. Woodard would be ready to return home on Sunday.

———

As it happened, the doctor was finished with his work in the area, so he and Joe left on Sunday.

"Don't forget to come to my school," Mandie

called to Joe as he climbed into the buggy. "Let me know when."

"I will," Joe promised and threw a kiss Mandie's way as Dr. Woodard got the vehicle moving.

The rest of the day was rushed for Mandie. Aunt Lou had finished the new dresses and other garments and had neatly packed them away in Mandie's trunk. Mandie left out her navy blue traveling suit to wear to school.

Monday morning before sunrise she was up and getting dressed because Mr. Bond had said they needed to get to the depot on time just in case the train was early. Mandie knew things never seemed to run on schedule with the railroad.

While she was dressing, there was a soft tap on Mandie's door, and it slipped open. Liza poked her head inside. "I didn't want to wake you but I sees you done up and gittin' dressed," the Negro girl said as she danced into the room.

"Come on in, Liza," Mandie said as she searched among the trays and ornate jewelry boxes on her dresser. "I'm looking for my locket." She pulled a chain out, and the gold heart on the end of it came into sight. "Here it is," she added. She opened the face of the locket and gazed at the only picture she had of her father.

Liza came to her side and said, "Heah, Missy 'Manda. Lemme fasten dat on fo' you."

Mandie turned to show the girl the photo. "That's my father," she said in a shaky voice.

"I knows," Liza said softly. "Now, let me fasten it round yo' neck so's you don't lose it." She reached for the locket as Mandie closed its face.

"Be sure you get the clasp closed tight. I don't want to lose it," Mandie told her.

Liza fastened the chain and stood back. "Now you all fixed up. 'Ceptin' dat white cat. Whut you plannin' to do wid dat animal?"

Mandie looked at Liza in surprise and said, "Do with him? Why—" She hesitated. She had not made plans for Snowball, but she quickly made up her mind. "Why, I'll just take Snowball with me."

Liza danced around the room and shook her head. "You knows dat school woman don't like no cat now."

"I'll take him with me and leave him at Grandmother's house. She'll keep him for me, and that way I can see him when I visit Grandmother," Mandie decided.

"Better ask yo' mama," Liza warned her.

"Oh, she'll agree," Mandie predicted.

And Elizabeth did agree for Mandie to take Snowball with her. Mr. Bond would leave Snowball with her grandmother after he left Mandie at the school.

When the train arrived in Asheville, Uncle Cal from the school was waiting. He had been meeting every train as the students arrived, taking them and their luggage to the school.

Mandie rushed off the train ahead of Mr. Bond, and even with Snowball in her arms, she managed to give Uncle Cal a quick hug.

"I'm so glad to see you, Uncle Cal. How's Aunt Phoebe?" Mandie asked.

"She be all right, even if'n dat Miz Prudence try to work her to death to git dat school more den spotless," the old Negro man replied as he helped Mr. Bond get Mandie's luggage and load it in the school rig. "Fo' two weeks now, all's we kin heah is 'Git dat flo' mopped, straighten dat curtain, move dat chair, wash dem bedspreads, go, go, go,' mawnin' to dark, jes' to put on airs fo' de parents whut be comin' wid de girls to start school.''

Mandie frowned as she listened to Uncle Cal. She had never heard him complain about anything before. Miss Prudence really must be on an unreasonable streak to stir up the old man so much. Mandie loved him and his wife, Aunt Phoebe, and she didn't like seeing them mistreated.

Mandie reached to touch Uncle Cal's sleeve as Mr. Bond gave her his hand to step up into the rig and said, "Don't worry about it, Uncle Cal. I am going to ask my grandmother to buy the school, and I know when she does she won't be mean to y'all." She sat down with Snowball in her lap behind Uncle Cal, and Mr. Bond took the seat next to the old man.

Uncle Cal glanced back and said, "I doubts you kin git yo' grandma to do dat." Then motioning to Snowball, he added, "You knows dat Miz Prudence, she don't want no cat in her school."

"I know, Uncle Cal. Don't worry about it. Mr. Jason is going to take him to my grandmother's house as soon as he leaves me at school," Mandie explained.

"That is *if* Uncle Cal will be good enough to take me by there on my way back to get the train home," Mr. Bond said with a smile.

"Oh, dat I will, dat I will," Uncle Cal promised.

When they arrived at the school, Uncle Cal drew the rig up to the front door. He and Mr. Bond unloaded Mandie's luggage and placed it in the front hallway. There were already several other trunks and bags sitting there, and a few of the students were standing around the foyer. Mandie quickly looked about for her friend Celia Hamilton, but there was no sign of her. Then Mandie remembered Celia's train probably wouldn't arrive until later.

"You be a nice young lady, Miss Amanda, and I'll see you when you come back home," Mr. Bond told her as he gave her a quick squeeze around her shoulders.

Mandie clasped his big hand and promised, "I will, Mr. Jason." She held out Snowball to him and said, "Thank you for bringing me and taking Snowball to my grandmother's." She smiled up at him. He was Uncle John's caretaker, and he was the first one Mandie had met when she had come to her uncle John's house to live after her father died.

Mr. Bond took Snowball, and Uncle Cal motioned for him to get in. When Mr. Bond joined him in the rig, Mandie stood on the huge veranda waving goodbye until they disappeared down the road. Then she turned and reentered the front hallway.

Mandie looked around and didn't see anyone she cared to talk to. "I'll just sit here and wait for Celia to arrive or for Uncle Cal to come back and take my trunk upstairs," she said to herself as she sat down in a big upholstered chair in an alcove. The long, floor-length windows gave a clear view of the front driveway, where Celia would arrive.

Suddenly Mandie remembered something. She did not know which room would be assigned to her this year. How would she find out? She got up and walked around the huge hallway as she looked for Miss Prudence or Miss Hope, the schoolmistresses.

She finally spotted Miss Hope stepping into the hallway from the office and going in the opposite direction. Mandie ran to catch up with her.

"Miss Hope!" she called. "Miss Hope, could I ask you something?"

Miss Hope stopped upon hearing her and turned around to wait for Mandie to catch up. "Did you have a nice vacation, dear?" she asked as Mandie stopped alongside her.

"Oh yes, ma'am, I'll tell you all about it when you have time, but right now would you please tell me what room I'll be in this year and who my roommate will be? Please, please let it be Celia."

"Why, of course, you and Celia will room together this year in the same room you had last year. Did your grandmother not tell you?" Miss Hope asked with a big smile.

Mandie grabbed the lady's hand, squeezed it, and said, "Oh, thank you, thank you, Miss Hope. No, my grandmother hasn't told me because I haven't seen her since I came back home from visiting Uncle Ned and Sallie."

"Well, you know how it is," Miss Hope said, still smiling. "My sister Prudence always likes to please our biggest benefactors and, of course, your grandmother is our most generous one. She stopped by last week, and we made arrangements then for you and Celia to continue on in the same room."

"I'm so thankful, Miss Hope. You see, my next-door neighbor, Polly Cornwallis, is coming to school here this year and she wanted to share a room with me. But I didn't want to do that because Celia is my best friend."

"Yes, I met Mrs. Cornwallis and Polly when they came to register. Now, dear, I have lots to do so I'll see you later. Just tell Uncle Cal to take your things and Celia's to your old room." Miss Hope smiled as she turned and hurried on down the corridor.

Mandie went back to the foyer to watch for her friend Celia. While she stood looking out the window, she heard Miss Prudence speak in an angry voice to Aunt Phoebe. She turned around to see what was going on.

"You know we have all the parents coming in here today and that the place must be absolutely spotless. Now, be sure you keep it that way." Miss Prudence was standing in the hallway facing Aunt Phoebe, who was carrying a mop and bucket.

"Yessum, yessum, it stay dat way," Aunt Phoebe said as Miss Prudence walked on down the hallway. The old Negro woman wiped up a spot on the shiny parquet floor with her mop.

As soon as Miss Prudence disappeared, Mandie ran to greet Aunt Phoebe.

"Aunt Phoebe, I'm so glad to see you again," Mandie said, reaching to embrace the old woman.

"I'se glad to be seein' you, too, Missy, but right now I'se got work to do," Aunt Phoebe said as she stepped away from Mandie. "You git on wid yo' bidniss whilst I does mine now."

Mandie was surprised. She had never seen Aunt Phoebe so upset before. And Uncle Cal had been short-tempered, too. Evidently Miss Prudence was on what the students called "her warpath."

"I'm sorry, Aunt Phoebe. I'll see you later when you get caught up," Mandie said as she turned away.

"You be's sho' you does dat," Aunt Phoebe said with half a smile as she glanced up at Mandie from the floor she was cleaning.

"I will," Mandie promised as she walked back to the front of the hallway.

Just as Mandie reached the window to look out again, she was shocked to see Uncle Cal pull up in the rig with Snowball in his arms and with no sign of Mr. Bond. She quickly met the old man on the front porch.

"What happened?" Mandie asked. "Why did you bring Snowball back?"

"I tuck Mistuh Bond to de depot and den tuck dis Snowball to yo' grandma's, but ain't no sign of nobody at huh house, so I hads to bring him back heah. Miz Prudence, she gwine raise de roof when she see him," the old man said as he handed the squirming white cat to Mandie.

She took Snowball and held him tightly in her arms. "Oh, Uncle Cal, what am I going to do? I wonder where my grandmother is? I would think some of the servants would have been at the house," Mandie complained.

"Sorry, Missy, I dones de best I could. Now I got to git de luggage upstairs," he said, going through the front door to survey the bags sitting around the hallway that would have to be carried to rooms upstairs.

Mandie followed him and said, "But, Uncle Cal, you can't handle all these by yourself up those stairs."

"I knows. But I got help," the old man told her, and he pointed toward a young Negro man coming toward them. "Miss Prudence done borrowed Chuck heah fo' de day from Mistuh Chadwick, whut runs de boys' school."

Mandie stepped out of the way and watched as the two men carried trunks and other bags up the winding staircase. Then she remembered her own small bag that held all her jewelry and special little items. She wanted to carry that bag herself and save the men from having to take it up. Still holding

Snowball tightly in her arms, she located the bag and picked it up.

Afraid of what would happen if Miss Prudence saw Snowball, Mandie went to sit in an alcove, out of sight from the hallway. From there, she could still watch through the window for Celia. She held Snowball in her lap and put the bag on the floor by the chair. Mandie feared an unpleasant confrontation with Miss Prudence and she kept trying to figure out how to solve her problem.

Chapter 3 / Where Is Grandmother Taft?

Uncle Cal and Chuck had taken most of the girls' luggage to their rooms by the time Mandie finally saw Celia and her aunt Rebecca step down from a hired hack. Uncle Cal saw them at the same time and rushed outside to bring their luggage inside.

Mandie knocked on the windowpane in an effort to get Celia's attention, but without success. She was afraid to step out into the main front hallway because Miss Prudence might see Snowball. So when she heard the front screen door open, then shut, she stuck her head around the corner and hissed at Celia.

"Celia!" Mandie said in a loud whisper, motioning to her friend to come into the alcove.

Celia looked at Mandie in surprise and came

toward her. "What's the matter?" Celia asked in a loud voice.

"Sh-h-h-h!" Mandie warned her, holding a finger at her own lips. "Come in here. Quick!"

Celia looked back at her aunt and said, "I'll be back, Aunt Rebecca, by the time you check into the office."

"All right, dear," the lady said as she continued on down the hallway toward the office.

Mandie reached for Celia's hand and pulled her into the alcove. "I'm in trouble," she said.

"Oh, Mandie! Not already!" Celia said with a moan as she looked at Snowball in Mandie's arms.

"It's Snowball," Mandie explained. "You see, Mr. Jason and I brought him with us, and Mr. Jason went on back home. Uncle Cal went by my grandmother's to leave Snowball, but there's no one at her home. So I'm stuck."

"Well, you can't stay in here all day," Celia reminded her. "I'd say you just better explain things to Miss Prudence."

"No, Miss Prudence is on the warpath. She is being mean and unreasonable with Aunt Phoebe about keeping the place clean," Mandie said. "And guess what? Polly Cornwallis is coming to school here. She won't be in until tomorrow, but she wanted to share a room with me. I told her no. I asked Miss Hope when I got here, before Uncle Cal brought Snowball back, and she said that you and I were to have the same room we had last year. Isn't that great?"

"Oh, I'm so glad, Mandie. I've been worrying about where they would put me this year," Celia said. "But, Mandie, I'm going to have to go. My aunt Rebecca will be here for a little while, until the next train goes back to Richmond."

"Your train must have been awfully late coming in, wasn't it?" Mandie asked.

"Terribly late, and I'm terribly hot and tired. I'd like to get out of these traveling clothes," Celia said as she glanced down at the brown traveling suit she had on. She leaned back and took a look into the hallway. "I see Aunt Rebecca coming back now, and she'll want to rest in our room until it's time for her to leave."

Aunt Rebecca had spotted Celia and she came to the corner of the alcove. "Well, hello, Amanda dear," the lady said. "I see you brought your cat to school with you."

Mandie quickly explained about the cat.

"Well, it's not your fault really," Aunt Rebecca said. "If I were you, I'd ask Uncle Cal to check at your grandmother's again. If there's still no one at her house, I'd take the cat up to your room and keep him shut in there until your grandmother does come home."

"That's a good idea, Aunt Rebecca," Mandie said as Snowball squirmed to get down. "Y'all go ahead up to our room, and I'll come up as soon as I can."

While Celia and Aunt Rebecca went upstairs, Mandie stayed in the alcove watching for Uncle Cal. There was more luggage sitting in the hallway, but he had not been back in a while. Then she saw three boys from Mr. Chadwick's School for Boys bring in several cartons.

"Let's bring those books into the office, please, boys," Miss Prudence called to them from down the hallway.

They followed her, and Mandie didn't see them

come back out, but she thought it was because she was trying to watch the front door, too. The school rig was not outside, so evidently Uncle Cal was out with it.

In a little while, Mandie saw Uncle Cal pull up in front in the rig with April Snow and Etrulia Batson. The two girls stepped down and came inside. Mandie watched until the old Negro began bringing the luggage into the hallway, and then she slipped out of the alcove long enough to speak to him.

"Uncle Cal, when you have time on one of your trips to the depot, would you please circle by my grandmother's again and see if there's anyone there yet?" Mandie asked. "I don't know what to do with Snowball."

"Sorry, Missy, but I been gwine by dat house ev'ry trip 'cause it be almost on de way to de depot, but ain't nobody home yet. I'll keep checkin'," the old man told her as he went back outside.

"Thank you," Mandie called after him as she stepped back into the alcove.

Mandie knew it would soon be time for supper, and she would have to be present at the table. She was also feeling more and more uncomfortable in her traveling suit. She saw Uncle Cal return twice more, but he just shook his head at her as he unloaded luggage.

"Snowball, we're going to have to take a chance on getting you to our room," she told the white cat. She glanced into the hallway. No one was in sight. *Evidently the students have all gone to their rooms,* she thought, *and the schoolmistresses must be in their office.* "Now's the time," she added in a whisper as she stepped into the hallway and headed toward the stairs.

Mandie had already put her foot on the first step when she remembered her little bag sitting on the floor near the chair in the alcove. She quickly turned back to get it, picked it up, and started back toward the steps. For some reason Snowball suddenly became brave and managed to jump out of her arms. Mandie put the bag down in the hallway and went after the cat.

"Come back here, Snowball!" Mandie whispered angrily, trying to watch the hallway while she retrieved him from under the stairs. She had left his leash and collar on and was able to step on the end of the leash as he crawled away.

Snowball hissed and fought with her.

"I think I know what's wrong," Mandie said with a moan. "Come on. I'll take you outside on the grass."

She picked him up, hurried out the front door, and set him down quickly in the yard, holding firmly to the end of the leash. Sure enough, Snowball had only been looking for a sandbox. He scratched up dirt in the grass and used the spot where he'd dug.

"Now, we're going to my room and no fuss about it," Mandie told him as he allowed her to pick him up.

Mandie slipped back into the front hallway and looked around. There was no one in sight. She picked up her little bag from the spot she had left it, and was about to rush up the steps when she felt something wet on her ankle. Glancing down, she was shocked to see brown fluid dripping from the bag. She was puzzled because she had no liquid in her bag.

At that precise moment, Miss Prudence came into the hallway from the office. Mandie moved ahead to the first step and turned so Miss Prudence couldn't see Snowball in her arms. Now the bag was dripping on the stairway. Mandie kept watching the drips and looking back at the schoolmistress. She didn't think she could get all the way up the steps fast enough to get out of sight, so she just stood on the step.

Miss Prudence immediately spotted the brown puddle on the parquet floor and yelled at Aunt Phoebe, who was carrying a bucket and mop as she came down the hallway. "I told you to keep this front hall spotless. Parents will be in and out all day. Now get this cleaned up. At once!" she said sharply as she motioned toward the spot.

Aunt Phoebe stared in surprise when she saw the mess and said, "Yessum."

The old Negro woman bent over to mop as Miss Prudence disappeared back down the hallway. Evidently the schoolmistress had not noticed Mandie.

"I knows I dun cleaned dis heah flo'. I knows I has. And lawsy mercy, if this don't be some sticky kinda mess," Aunt Phoebe said as she rubbed hard at the stuff.

Mandie watched silently, not knowing what to do. Finally Aunt Phoebe looked up and saw her. She noticed the drip from Mandie's bag, but Mandie didn't say a word.

"Whut you dun got in dat bag, Missy? It be ruinin' de whole flo'," Aunt Phoebe said to her.

"I don't know, Aunt Phoebe," Mandie said as she finally plopped down on the step.

"Den you bettuh be findin' out 'cause I ain't gwine mop and mop and re-mop dis heah flo' all day," Aunt Phoebe said sternly, straightening up to look at Mandie.

Mandie was paralyzed with fear. Things were all so strange and she couldn't reply.

"Look in dat bag, Missy, right now, you heah?" Aunt Phoebe demanded as she started toward Mandie.

Mandie tried to open the bag, but the hook was stuck. In the rush, Snowball managed to get away again. She let him go because she was so disgusted with everything and so tired that she just didn't care what would happen if Miss Prudence saw Snowball.

Aunt Phoebe snatched the bag away from Mandie and managed to jerk open the hook. Mandie snatched the bag back and dumped it onto the steps. Aunt Phoebe stood there, angrily fussing as Mandie's jewelry spilled out and a jar of what looked like molasses tumbled out, too. The lid was missing, and Aunt Phoebe caught it before the jar emptied itself on the stairs.

"I didn't bring any molasses in this bag! I didn't! I didn't!" Mandie cried as she surveyed the mess.

"Well, it sho' got in dere somehow. Now git all dat junk outta my way so's I kin clean up de mess 'fo' dat Miz Prudence see it," Aunt Phoebe demanded.

Tears streamed down Mandie's cheeks. She pulled up her skirt and picked up the jewelry and trinkets piece by piece and dropped them in her lap. Everything was sticky, and her skirt became a mess. When she had dropped it all on her skirt, she pulled up the hem and turned to race upstairs without another word.

Running blindly into the bathroom, Mandie dumped the whole mess into the big bathtub and turned on the water. She sat down on the floor and cried. *Who has done this to me?* she thought. *And why? Why?*

She had not seen anyone go near the bag, but she remembered leaving it unattended on the floor several times. Anyone could have seen it and dropped the jar of molasses inside. *But why?* she wondered.

There was a soft knock, which Mandie ignored. The door was pushed slowly open, and Mandie looked up to see Celia standing there. Celia rushed to her side and stooped down.

"Mandie, what's wrong?" she asked, anxiously grabbing Mandie's hand in hers and then realizing it was all sticky. "What is this stuff?" Celia asked. Then she saw the jewelry in the water in the bathtub. "Mandie, everything's going to ruin." Celia started picking the pieces out of the water, washing them as she did, and laying them in the lavatory.

After a moment, Mandie reached for a piece of toilet paper and wiped her eyes. Standing up, she unbuttoned her skirt and dropped the sticky mess to the floor. Between sobs she told Celia, "Somebody put an open jar of molasses in my bag."

Celia was shocked. Mandie tried to explain.

"And what did you do with Snowball?" Celia asked.

"Oh no, he got away and I forgot about him," Mandie cried, tears flowing again.

"I hung up your clothes for you when Uncle Cal brought up your trunk," Celia said. "Take off the rest of that sticky mess and I'll go get you something clean to put on," Celia told her. "Aunt Rebecca just left to catch the train, so I'll go with you to look for Snowball. Now hurry." She left the bathroom and closed the door behind her.

Mandie shed the rest of the sticky garments and washed up. When she looked in the mirror, she saw how red her eyes looked and she tried to stop crying. Celia brought her a pink voile dress and clean underwear. While Mandie dressed, Celia took the jewelry and trinkets out of the lavatory and dried them. Mandie looked at her locket on the chain around her neck, glad it had not been soiled.

"I suppose I ruined my traveling suit," Mandie said as she gingerly picked up a corner of her skirt from the floor.

"You need to ask Uncle Cal to take it to the pressing club. They can get it clean," Celia assured her. "I spilled something on my clothes once, and the pressing club near my house made them look like new."

Mandie rolled the clothes up into a bundle and carried them into their room. Celia brought the jewelry that she had gathered into a big towel.

"I suppose I'd better look for Snowball," Mandie said with a loud moan. "And I suppose it's about time for supper, isn't it?" She squinted at the clock Celia had placed on the table. She had a headache, and her eyes hurt so much she could hardly see.

"In about thirty minutes," Celia said. "Come on. We've got time to find Snowball before the supper bell rings." She led the way out into the hallway.

They went down the curving staircase and saw several other students coming and going, but Mandie avoided looking at them because she knew her face was a sight.

"He got away from me at the bottom of the staircase when Aunt Phoebe caught up with me and that bag," Mandie explained.

The two girls hurried through every hallway and

looked into each empty classroom. As they passed the office door, Mandie noticed that both Miss Prudence and Miss Hope were inside working at their desks. The schoolmistresses didn't notice the girls as they went by.

Finally, Mandie said, "The only place left to look is in the kitchen, and I hate to go in there because Aunt Phoebe is angry with me." She stopped and stared at the closed door.

Celia laughed and started toward the door as she said, "Well, you know Snowball. If there is one bite of food around, he'll find it." She pushed the door open, and Mandie followed her into the kitchen.

Aunt Phoebe and Millie were so busy with pots and pans on the big iron cookstove that they didn't notice the girls.

Uncle Cal saw them as he came in through the back door with an armload of wood for the stove. He looked at Mandie and said, "Missy, I done been back to yo' grandma's agin and der still ain't nobody home."

As Uncle Cal placed the wood in a box nearby, Aunt Phoebe and Millie turned quickly to see whom he was talking to.

"Now whut you two young ladies be doin' in dis heah kitchen? You knows dat ain't 'lowed," Aunt Phoebe said.

"I'm sorry, Aunt Phoebe, but I'm looking for Snowball. He got away from me because of that mess," Mandie said in an uncertain tone. She was afraid the old woman would yell at her again.

"Dat cat musta bin in de kitchen 'cause dere's fried chicken missing from top of de stove," Aunt Phoebe said. "And de last I seed of him he wuz hightailin' it t'ward de office room whut Miz Hope stay in to work." She turned to stir the contents of a big pot. "Now y'all git yoselfs outta heah 'fo' somebody find you heah. Soon be time to eat."

"Thank you, Aunt Phoebe, but if y'all happen to see him will you please catch him and hold him for me?" Mandie asked.

"We'll try," Aunt Phoebe said. She started fanning her hands toward the door. "Shoo now! Git outta heah!"

Mandie and Celia left the kitchen quickly and glanced around the hallway outside the door to make sure there was no one in sight. They walked on down the corridor, and when they passed the office door, Mandie noticed that the two schoolmistresses were no longer inside.

"Snowball, are you in there?" Mandie whispered as she stuck her head inside the office. She slipped inside to look around. Celia followed. There were lots of papers lying on the desks, and the wire wastebasket seemed to be full of crumpled paper. Mandie was about to leave when the wastebasket suddenly moved. She stepped closer and saw Snowball uncurling and stretching, evidently waking from a nap. Mandie reached down and snatched him up.

"Oh, you crazy cat—of all places to hide," Mandie scolded him as she held tight to the red leash.

"Well, at least we found him," Celia said. "I'll run and stick my head in the kitchen door to let Aunt Phoebe know we found him. Be right back." She raced down the corridor.

Mandie turned to leave the room but, at that moment, Miss Prudence suddenly appeared in the doorway. She was shocked to see Mandie in her office.

"Well, just what are you doing here?" Miss Prudence asked as she stepped up in front of Mandie. And before Mandie could answer, the headmistress saw the white cat. "And what are you doing with that animal in my school? You know that is not allowed. Speak up, young lady."

"I'm sorry, Miss Prudence," Mandie began in a trembly voice. "I brought Snowball with me from home and was going to leave him with my grandmother, but nobody is at her house, and the cat got away from me when I found the molasses and—"

Miss Prudence interrupted, "I'm not asking for your life history, young lady. You will have to do something with that cat immediately. I won't have him in my school. Now, what were you up to in my office here?"

"I was just looking for Snowball," Mandie said, "and I found him asleep in there." She pointed nervously to the wastebasket.

Miss Prudence scrutinized Mandie's face. "Did you look at any of the papers on my desk?" she asked.

"Oh no, Miss Prudence, I wouldn't do that. No, ma'am," Mandie assured her.

"All the students in this school have been informed and know perfectly well that the offices are strictly off limits unless you are invited in," Miss Prudence reminded her. "You will report to me here right after the evening meal. And you should have a solution to the presence of that cat by then."

Mandie backed out the door as she said, "Yes, ma'am." She bumped into Celia in the hallway. Taking Celia's hand, she rushed down the corridor toward the front staircase.

Finally stopping for a breath at the steps, Mandie explained what had happened. "At least she didn't catch you in the office," Mandie said.

"But I was in there, same as you. Maybe I ought to tell her I was," Celia said, frowning.

"No, no, no," Mandie objected. "What good would it do? You'd only be in trouble too. No, just don't tell anyone you were in there."

"Well, if you say so. But I feel guilty knowing I should have been reprimanded same as you," Celia said as they continued up the staircase.

When the two girls entered their room, Mandie suddenly realized the cat would have to have a sandbox to stay there.

"I have to get a sandbox for Snowball, Celia," Mandie said. "I'll be right back. I'll ask Uncle Cal to get some sand for me so at least I won't be caught doing that."

Mandie rushed out the door and down the back stairway, which came out near the back door. She stopped and listened to find out who was in the kitchen. She could hear Uncle Cal chopping wood in the backyard. She wouldn't have to go through the kitchen if she hurried. Pushing back the latch on the door, she ran outside into the yard.

Uncle Cal stopped working as she rushed up to speak to him.

"Uncle Cal, I found Snowball but I need a sandbox for him in my room until I can do something with him," Mandie told him. "Would you please help me?"

"You jes' leave it to me, Missy. I'll bring a box shortly," the old man told her. "Now, Missy, go back inside 'fo' you gits late for suppuh." He set down his ax and walked toward the shed in the backyard.

Mandie called, "Thank you," rushed back into the house, and up to her room. Snowball was curled up asleep on the bed. Celia was relaxing in a big chair.

"Uncle Cal is bringing a sandbox, thank goodness," Mandie said as she plopped into a nearby chair. "Oh, what a terrible day!" She sighed loudly.

"Do you not have any idea who might have put that jar of molasses in your bag?" Celia asked.

"No, and I can't imagine how they had an opportunity to do it," Mandie said. "There were other people around, and it looks to me like they should have been afraid someone would see them. Besides, I didn't leave the bag alone very long at a time."

"What are you going to do with Snowball? Miss Prudence said you have to make plans for him by the time you talk to her after supper," Celia said.

"There's nothing I can do with him until my grandmother comes home. I just don't understand why there's absolutely no one at her house," Mandie pondered, "and she didn't tell me she wouldn't be home when I got here."

"Maybe she needed a vacation after that long journey with us," Celia said with a laugh. "We certainly weren't very well behaved a lot of the time."

"Oh, my grandmother is used to that. She knows me well enough," Mandie replied. She got up to walk around the room. "You know, Hilda was supposed to come back to my grandmother's house when we returned from Europe. Grandmother left her with friends until she could come back."

"Well, I suppose if Uncle Cal will continue

checking there when he's out with the rig he'll eventually find out something," Celia said.

Mandie suddenly remembered the other reason she wanted to see her grandmother. She stopped walking and looked at her friend. "Celia, I need to see her as soon as possible. I'm going to ask her to buy this school so we won't have to go somewhere else or get some disagreeable new owners," she said.

"Your grandmother? Buy this school?" Celia asked in surprise.

"My mother and Uncle John both think she might agree to do it," Mandie said. "They said she owns so many other things that one more wouldn't matter to her. She has all these business people working for her to take care of everything."

"I just can't imagine your grandmother buying this school," Celia said.

"If she doesn't, there's no telling what might happen to it," Mandie said with a deep sigh. "And we need to think up another plan if she won't buy it."

"My mother and I talked about the news that the Heathwoods want to sell it," Celia said. "She thinks they're probably running out of money, that they aren't charging enough to cover their expenses or something."

There was a knock on the door and Mandie opened it to find Uncle Cal standing there with a box of sand.

"Where we gwine put dis now?" he asked Mandie.

"Oh, over there in the corner will be fine, Uncle Cal," Mandie told him as she motioned to a corner in the room. "And I appreciate this so much."

The supper bell in the backyard began ringing, and the girls left the old man to find a place for the box while they rushed downstairs to get in line for supper. Mandie knew she wouldn't be able to eat much with the interview with Miss Prudence hanging over her head.

Chapter 4 / More Trouble

Mandie and Celia were on the schedule for the first seating at meals. The dining room couldn't accommodate the entire student body at once, so Miss Prudence presided over the table at the first seating and watched each girl. Her sister, Miss Hope, was in charge of the second seating.

To Mandie's relief, she and Celia were to sit next to each other as they had the previous school year. But April Snow was also in her former place—directly across from Mandie. Mandie tried to smile at the girl who was always causing trouble, but April pushed back her long, black hair and stared at Mandie with her deep, black eyes.

The girls stood behind their chairs and waited for Miss Prudence to return thanks. The lady picked up a little silver bell by her plate at the head of the table and shook it. "Order, girls," she commanded.

The head schoolmistress watched to see that every head was bowed and then spoke, "We thank

Thee, dear God, for this food of which we are about to partake, and ask Thy blessings on it and on all who are present. Amen." As the girls raised their heads she continued, "Please be seated, and be as ladylike as you can make it."

Miss Prudence quickly sat down, then watched as the students took their seats. Mandie noticed that most of the girls were able to scoot into their chairs without making hardly any noise. The girls at this table had almost all been at the school the previous year, and Mandie knew they realized how strict Miss Prudence could be.

Millie, the maid, had already placed the food on the table, and now she moved around the room filling glasses with water and bringing more hot biscuits from the sideboard. She stopped at Mandie's side, smiled, and whispered, "I'se glad you is back, Missy." Millie watched Miss Prudence carefully to see if she saw her talking. "I feed de white cat in yo' room."

"I'm glad to be back, Millie," Mandie said under her breath as the maid moved quickly on. "Thanks."

Evidently Uncle Cal had told Millie that Snowball was in Mandie's room. Mandie felt a strong wave of love surge through her heart for the Negro servants at the school. She loved them all and they always looked out for her.

Then she caught her breath as she remembered she would have to meet with Miss Prudence after the meal, and she still didn't know what she would do with Snowball.

No conversation was allowed at the table, but Mandie saw Celia glance at her as she pushed the food around on her plate. Mandie couldn't eat much while worrying about what the schoolmistress would do. She hoped for a chance to ask Uncle Cal if he had checked on her grandmother again. *Maybe he might know something by now*, she thought. But as Mandie watched Miss Prudence rise and dismiss the girls from the table, she motioned for Mandie to follow her to the office.

Conversation could begin again as soon as the girls walked into the hallway, and Mandie said to Celia, "Well, I have to go now. Will you wait for me on the front porch? Please."

"Of course, Mandie, I'll be there," Celia said. She continued down the corridor leading to the front door and Mandie headed for the office.

Miss Prudence was already sitting behind her desk as Mandie entered the room. "Come on in now, Amanda," the lady told her. "Sit there." She motioned to a straight chair, and as Mandie silently sat, Miss Prudence continued speaking, "Now, what have you done with that white cat?"

"He's in my room, Miss Prudence. You see, my grandmother is still not at home, and I don't have anywhere to put him until she gets back from wherever she's gone," Mandie explained. She practically held her breath, anticipating a reprimand.

"You know that is not allowed, Amanda," Miss Prudence said quickly with a deep frown. "Just where is your grandmother? She came by here last week and didn't say anything about leaving town."

"I'm sorry, Miss Prudence, but I don't know. Uncle Cal said even the servants were gone when he checked at her home for me," Mandie said as she, too, frowned. "As soon as she gets back home, I know she'll take Snowball for me."

"And just suppose she has gone on an extended

journey and won't return for several days, or even several weeks. What do you plan on doing with that cat?" Miss Prudence asked her.

"I could write a letter to my mother and ask her to send someone to get him, but that would take a while to do," Mandie suggested. "But really, Miss Prudence, Snowball is a good cat. He's not bothering anyone as long as he stays in my room."

Miss Prudence tapped on her desk with a pencil as she replied, "It isn't a case of whether the cat is a good cat or not. It's a case of rules being broken, Amanda." The lady suddenly raised her eyes and spoke to someone behind Mandie outside in the hallway. "Yes, what is it? I'm busy right now," she said sharply.

Before the other person replied, Mandie knew it had to be Aunt Phoebe, because Miss Prudence seemed to be continually fussing with the black woman.

"Excuse me, Miz Prudence," Aunt Phoebe said as Mandie glanced around to look at the servant. "I jes' wanted to say I done tuck dat white cat out to my house in de backyard and me and Cal, we gwine keep him for Missy 'Manda till huh grandma come home."

Mandie jumped up and ran to squeeze Aunt Phoebe's hand as she said, "Oh, thank you, Aunt Phoebe. Thank you."

"Amanda!" Miss Prudence said loudly. "You are not dismissed and you will sit back down until I am finished with you."

Mandie quickly went back to her chair and, as she glanced back to Aunt Phoebe, noticed that the old woman had already vanished down the hallway.

"Now that we have that temporarily solved, I

need to get to this other problem. I understand from Aunt Phoebe that you had molasses in a bag and let it drip out all over the front hallway," Miss Prudence said, frowning at Mandie. "And I want you to know that we will not put up with such things. Do you understand?"

"But, Miss Prudence, I didn't even know the molasses was in my bag," Mandie protested. "It wasn't in the bag when I got here from home today. Somebody put it in there."

"Amanda!" Miss Prudence again tapped her desk with the pencil. "You do not accuse someone else for your misdemeanors. You are off to a bad start this year, and if anything else happens, please remember that we will take stringent measures. Now you may go." Standing up, she dropped the pencil onto her desk.

Mandie quickly rose and said, "I understand, Miss Prudence. Thank you."

She hurried out into the hallway and rushed toward the front porch to find Celia. Miss Prudence never cared to hear the other side of an argument. Mandie knew that from past experience. Fortunately, she had not been punished for something that was not her fault. Somebody had put that jar of molasses in her bag to cause her trouble, and now it was up to her to find out who.

When she pushed open the front screen door, Celia was talking to Etrulia Batson at the corner of the porch. Celia saw Mandie and quickly came to join her.

"Let's walk," Mandie said to her friend as she went down the front steps. Celia followed.

When they were out of hearing of the other girls on the porch, Celia whispered, "What happened?"

"You know Miss Prudence," Mandie said with a big sigh as they sat on a bench under a huge magnolia tree. "She wouldn't listen to me when I told her I hadn't put the molasses in my bag and messed everything up."

"Is she going to punish you?" Celia asked.

"I don't think so. She didn't say she would, but she reminded me that if anything else happens she will," Mandie explained. Then she remembered Snowball. "Oh, guess what! Aunt Phoebe took Snowball out to her house to stay until Grandmother comes home."

"She did? But I thought you said Aunt Phoebe seemed to be angry with you when your bag leaked on her clean floor," Celia said, pushing back her long auburn hair.

"Oh, she definitely was, but she just gave me a warning about anything else happening," Mandie said as she stood up. "Let's walk. I can't sit still."

Mandie looked down the hill on which the schoolhouse stood and glanced at the mountains in the distance. "Asheville, North Carolina, is a hilly town, isn't it?" she said as she and Celia strolled on.

"It sure is," Celia agreed. "But don't forget, we have terribly big mountains in Virginia where I live."

"I know, but so do we back home in Franklin," Mandie replied. She stopped to pluck a leaf from a shrub. "I wish my grandmother would come on back home. I want to ask her about buying this school. I'm afraid someone else will come to look at it, see the beautiful mountains, and decide to buy it."

"I'm not so sure the school will be sold that easily," Celia remarked. "Have you thought about the promise they made a long time ago that the school was going to get electric lights and a furnace? That has never happened. I imagine a buyer would want those things included."

Mandie turned to look at her friend. "You're right," she said. "I had forgotten all about that. I wonder why they haven't had those installed."

"Probably because of the cost," Celia said. "I'm sure it would take a lot of money."

"Yes, and I suppose Miss Prudence and Miss Hope would not want to put money into the school for remodeling if they aren't sure they can get all the money out of it when they sell it," Mandie said as she sauntered about the bed of roses in the yard.

"I wonder when we'll be having the boys from Mr. Chadwick's school over?" Celia said, glancing at Mandie.

"Soon, I hope," Mandie said. "I want to talk to Tommy Patton about our school being for sale."

"And Robert Rogers too," Celia added. "But what will they be able to do?"

"Well, I don't want Miss Prudence to sell the school to some stranger while we're students here," Mandie said as they continued strolling about. "And I thought we might be able to prevent that somehow until I can talk to my grandmother about buying it."

Celia laughed and said, "But, Mandie, I don't see how we can *prevent* Miss Prudence from selling the school to whomever she wants."

Mandie grinned and said, "Oh, Celia, there are ways to cause prospective buyers to lose interest in it."

Celia gasped and said, "Mandie, you are not going to do something to get into trouble, are you? Remember, Miss Prudence warned you about that."

"I have some ideas, but I want to talk to Tommy

and Robert about this first," Mandie said with a grin. "I may need the boys' help."

"What are you planning on doing?" Celia asked as she stopped and faced Mandie.

"I don't know for sure yet," Mandie said. "But there must be things we can do to stop the sale."

"*We?*" Celia said quickly. "Don't count on getting me into trouble with you."

"That's all right. I'm sure the boys will help me," Mandie said with a shrug. She started back up the hill to the schoolhouse.

Celia hurried alongside her. "Mandie, please don't do anything to get into trouble," she begged.

Mandie stopped and stamped her foot. "Oh, Celia, I'm not going to get into trouble," she said. "And you don't have to get involved. But one thing I am going to do is find out who put that jar of molasses in my bag."

That caught Celia's attention. "I hope you can," Celia said. "It just wasn't fair at all for somebody to do that to you. But how are you going to find out who did it?"

"It had to be somebody who came into the hallway while my bag was sitting in the alcove," Mandie said. "The problem is, there were a lot of people coming in and out—parents, the girls, the boys with boxes of books from Mr. Chadwick's school. I just have to remember who all that included."

"That's going to be a job," Celia remarked.

"I thought maybe if I sat down and made a list of people I recall seeing that would help me remember everybody," Mandie said. "In fact, I think I'll go to our room and get some paper and a pencil and start right now."

"I think I'll stay down here awhile," Celia told

her as the two girls reached the front porch. Several of the other students were sitting or standing about talking.

"All right," Mandie said, reaching to open the front screen door. She turned back to Celia and said, "If you're going to be down here awhile, would you do me a favor? If you see Uncle Cal, would you please ask him if he has checked on my grandmother again to see if anyone is home yet?"

"Sure. If I see Uncle Cal, I'll come up and let you know if he has any news," Celia promised as she walked toward the corner of the porch.

Mandie hurried up to their room and pushed the door open. Her mind was trying to remember who had been in the front hallway when she had left the bag in the alcove.

She was thinking so hard that she didn't notice anything out of order until her shoes crunched on something on the floor. She looked down and gasped in horror at seeing the sand from Snowball's sandbox scattered all over the rug. The box was upside down in the corner where Uncle Cal had left it.

"Oh no!" she cried to herself. "Who did this? Who?"

Mandie stood there in shock for a few moments, and then realized she'd have to clean up the mess. But how? She puzzled over the problem. She couldn't ask Aunt Phoebe to clean up after her again, not after that mess with the molasses. Where in the world could she find a broom? The only brooms and mops and pails she had ever seen were kept in a small room next to the kitchen.

"How can I find something to clean this up?" she asked herself as she stepped back out of the sandy mess. "If Miss Prudence sees this, I'll be in real trouble."

Mandie looked about the room to see if anything else had been disturbed. Everything seemed to be in place. Her eyes stopped on her hairbrush lying on the bureau across the room.

"The hairbrush!" she exclaimed as she lifted her long skirts and reached for it. "Now all I need is something to brush it onto." She looked around the room again. "The pin tray," she said as she picked up a shallow silver tray and emptied the pins, needles, and thread onto the bureau.

Mandie quickly turned the sandbox upright and pulled up her long skirts as she knelt to begin the cleanup. It was a slow process with such small equipment. She became frustrated and sat back on her heels. "Just wait," she exclaimed angrily to herself. "I'll get whoever did this!"

At that moment there was a light tap on the door, and Mandie quickly looked up to see Aunt Phoebe coming in. Mandie tried to get up, but she slipped on the sand and sat hard on the floor.

"Lawsy mercy, Missy, whut you done now?" Aunt Phoebe asked as she surveyed the mess of sand everywhere.

Mandie managed to get up and said, "Oh, Aunt Phoebe, somebody dumped out Snowball's sandbox while I was downstairs. I just came back and found it."

Aunt Phoebe put her hands on her hips and said, "Missy, you don't hafta tell me a story. I'll git de broom and shovel and clean it up fo' you. I was jes' comin' to git dat sandbox to take it ovuh to my house fo' dat white cat."

"Aunt Phoebe!" Mandie said sternly. "I did not

make this mess! I was trying to clean it up before Miss Prudence found out about it.''

"No nevuh mind, Missy. I git de broom. Be right back," the old woman said as she quickly left the room.

Mandie angrily threw the silver hairbrush across the room. It missed the floor-length mirror standing in the corner by only a fraction of an inch. "I get blamed for everything! Nobody believes me!" she cried as she dropped into a big chair.

At that moment Celia came into the room and stopped in surprise when she stepped into the sand.

"What's happened now?" Celia asked as she looked at Mandie.

Mandie jumped up and walked around the room. "Somebody dumped out Snowball's sandbox," she said angrily. "And when I find out who did it, they're going to wish they hadn't done it!"

"My goodness!" Celia exclaimed, shaking off the hems of her long skirts. "Why would anyone do such a thing?" She looked at Mandie and asked, "It didn't just turn over, did it?"

Mandie stopped walking around and stamped her foot. "Celia! I told you—somebody dumped it out," she said sternly.

Before Celia could reply, Aunt Phoebe came in carrying her broom and shovel. Without a word she began sweeping up the sand and putting it back into the sandbox.

"Aunt Phoebe, I appreciate your doing this for me," Mandie said to the old woman.

Without glancing up, Aunt Phoebe told her, "Jes' don't go round makin' no mo' messes, else you gwine end up in trouble wid Miz Prudence."

Mandie sighed and gave up. There was no use

trying to convince Aunt Phoebe that she had not made the mess. Celia stood by silently watching, and no one spoke until the old woman had finished and was picking up the sandbox to take with her. Then Mandie said, "I really thank you, Aunt Phoebe, and I really appreciate your keeping Snowball for me."

Aunt Phoebe set the sandbox out in the hallway, came back, and picked up her broom and shovel. "'Night now," she muttered as she left the room.

"Good-night," Mandie and Celia both called after her.

"I just don't know what else can happen," Mandie said as she flopped down on the window seat and stared out into the twilight.

Celia joined her. "I'm sorry, Mandie, if I sounded as though I doubted you when you explained what happened," she said. "It was such a shock to see sand all over our rug."

"That's all right, Celia," Mandie said, still looking outside. "I'm beginning to think somebody doesn't like me, and I don't think I like them very much."

"I came up to tell you I saw Uncle Cal right after you left, and went back by your grandmother's. But there's still no one at home," Celia explained.

Mandie turned around to face her friend. "I just can't figure out where my grandmother is," she said. "I've never known her to go off and not leave any servants at the house."

"Uncle Cal said he'd check by there again when he goes to the depot in the morning to pick up some more students who are coming in," Celia said. "And we have to start classes tomorrow. Miss Prudence made an announcement after you came upstairs that our schedules will be handed to us at breakfast."

"I hope we'll be in the same classes this year," Mandie said. "And I'm glad we got this room again. It's so far from the other girls' rooms that we have a little privacy, but it also gives someone a chance to do things like dumping out the sandbox."

"You're right, but this room is near the back stairs, where you can slip out and meet Uncle Ned when he comes to visit, remember?" Celia reminded her.

"I wish I could talk to Uncle Ned about all this trouble that has been happening," Mandie said. "But he probably won't come to visit me for a couple of weeks."

"Well, I think I'll get ready for bed and then read awhile," Celia said as she rose and walked toward the chifferobe.

"I might as well, too," Mandie said. She stood up and yawned. "I guess I'm tired." She followed Celia to the chifferobe to hang up her clothes. She stopped suddenly as she remembered something. "Oh, Celia, Polly Cornwallis will be here tomorrow. I wonder which room they'll put her in."

"Probably down on the second floor in one of those huge rooms with all those girls," Celia said as she took down her nightclothes from a hanger. "Do you think she might stir up some trouble here like she does at home?"

"I doubt it," Mandie said as she stepped out of her skirt. "Anyway, I can't blame her for these things that have been happening to me because she's not here yet."

"No," Celia agreed as she slipped out of her dress and into her nightgown.

"But I'll find out who is responsible, just you wait and see," Mandie promised.

She thought it might take a while to uncover the culprits, but she was determined to expose the troublemakers. She just hoped they didn't do anything else to her before she solved the mystery.

Chapter 5 / A Terrible Possibility

After Mandie and Celia had dressed for bed, Celia curled up on her pillows with a book to read. Mandie decided she must make herself a list of people she had seen in the front hallway. Taking her notebook and a pencil, she sat down in one of the big chairs in their room.

"The boys bringing in the books from Mr. Chadwick's school," she began, thinking out loud. "Aunt Phoebe, Miss Prudence, Miss Hope, Aunt Rebecca, Celia, Uncle Cal, and Chuck from Mr. Chadwick's School, Mr. Jason Bond, Etrulia Batson, April Snow—April Snow! She is always causing trouble. Maybe she is guilty again." Looking up at Celia, Mandie said, "April Snow! Maybe she put the molasses in my bag and turned over Snowball's sandbox. What do you think?"

Celia looked up from her book and said, "Well, I know she has caused a lot of trouble before but,

Mandie, when would she have had a chance to do all this?''

"I don't know, but then when did anyone have a chance to do it?" Mandie replied thoughtfully. "Someone got a chance somehow."

"Yes, and I suppose April had as good a chance as anyone else did," Celia said.

"I know," Mandie said with a loud sigh. "I think the best thing I can do is just watch everyone from now on and keep notes about whom I see where."

"That will be some job," Celia told her.

"Most of the time, when we go from class to class, we have our notebooks with us, so I can just keep a sheet of paper inside and write down names as I see people. When I don't have my notebook with me, I'll put a piece of paper in my pocket," Mandie decided as she stood up and stretched.

At that moment, the huge iron bell in the backyard began ringing. Both girls jumped at the sudden sound, then laughed.

"We are back at school, and the bell tells us it's ten o'clock and time for all lights to be put out," Mandie said. She blew out the kerosene lamp by the chair where she had been sitting and then made a dive for the bed.

"Here goes this one," Celia said as she extinguished the lamp by the bed.

It was a clear, moonlit night, and therefore not very dark outside. Mandie looked around the room as she and Celia caught up on what they had been doing since they parted after their journey to Europe with Mandie's grandmother.

"I wonder when Joe will come to Asheville," Mandie said. "I hope it's soon."

"Don't forget," Celia reminded her. "Polly Cornwallis will be here at this school ready to pounce on him when he arrives."

"I'm not worried about her. Joe and Dr. Woodard will probably stay at my grandmother's house anyway, and you and I can go over there on weekends—if my grandmother ever gets back home again," Mandie said.

"Mandie, I know your grandmother will return home when she gets good and ready. You know her. She goes and comes when she wants to. That's the good thing about living alone," Celia said.

"Oh, don't forget, she doesn't live alone anymore. She has Hilda to take care of, remember?" Mandie said as she half sat up, resting back on her elbows.

Celia sat up and said, "Of course she has Hilda, but you know she has people she can leave Hilda with when she wants to go off, like when she took us to Europe. Maybe she's gone to get Hilda from those friends who kept her while we were gone."

"But all the servants are gone, too," Mandie said. "She wouldn't take all the servants with her to do that." She lay back down on the bed and rumpled up her pillow.

Celia yawned as she curled up on her side of the bed. " 'Night. Remember, we have to get up early because we are on the first sitting for breakfast, and that means seven-thirty sharp down in the dining room."

"Right," Mandie mumbled. " 'Night."

Both girls were tired, and quickly drifted off to sleep. But when the bell in the backyard rang for the students to get up the next morning, Mandie felt as though she had just gone to bed.

Mandie yawned as she took down a dress from

the chifferobe. "I think I'll go to bed early tonight," she mumbled.

"Me too," Celia agreed as she started dressing.

When they were finished and ready to go to the dining room, Mandie remembered her plan and turned back. "I have to get a piece of paper and a pencil to put in my pocket. We won't have our notebooks until we come back after breakfast to go to class," she said. She quickly pulled a sheet out of her notebook on the table, folded it, and tucked it and a pencil into her deep pocket on the full skirt of her dress.

Celia waited in the doorway. "Hurry, Mandie. We don't want to be late on our first morning of school," she urged her.

"I'm ready," Mandie said. The two girls rushed down the long corridor, and then descended the two flights of steps to the first floor.

Mandie drew in a deep breath at the foot of the stairs and said, "Whew! It's a long ways down from the third floor!"

"It's worth it, though. I'm glad we're not in one of those big rooms with so many girls," Celia replied.

They turned the corner in the downstairs hallway and joined the line of girls waiting to enter the dining room. Most of the students were talking in soft tones. This was permissible while they were in line, but once they went through the doorway, all talking was forbidden.

Mandie quickly took the paper from her pocket and folded it smaller so no one could see what she had. Glancing out of the corner of her eye, she jotted down the names of all the girls she could see. She knew their names because these students had all been here the year before, and some even longer. The new students would be put into the second sitting.

"I just remembered something," Mandie said to Celia. "Polly will be new here, so she will have to join the second group for meals. She won't be eating with us."

"You're right," Celia agreed. "But I don't think Polly has arrived yet. It's too early in the morning."

"No, she'll come on the same train in the afternoon that I took yesterday. The one in the morning is too early," Mandie said as she continued writing down names.

Suddenly the French doors were thrown open, and the girls began moving into the dining room, where they stopped to stand behind their assigned chairs. Mandie pushed the paper and pencil back into her pocket and glanced around the room to be sure she had listed everyone present.

After Miss Prudence returned thanks for the food and everyone was seated, she picked up the little silver bell by her plate and shook it, even though the room was already quiet.

"Young ladies," the schoolmistress began. "As I call your names, please come forward and get your schedule." She picked up a stack of papers from beside her plate and began.

Knowing they were not allowed to talk in the dining room, Mandie and Celia quickly exchanged schedules when they returned to their seats. Mandie smiled when she saw that the two of them would be together in their classes. Celia smiled back.

When she had finished, Miss Prudence beckoned to Millie at the sideboard to bring the biscuits and coffee. The food was already in covered dishes on the table, and Miss Prudence began passing the bowls and platters.

Because talking was not allowed at the table, the girls automatically ate fast and were soon finished.

Miss Prudence tinkled the little bell again when the meal was over and said, "Young ladies, we have six new students coming today. Remember how it was when you first came here. Most of you didn't know a single soul, so please make them feel at home. You are dismissed now."

All the girls hurried out of the dining room. Mandie and Celia stopped for a moment in the hallway to compare their schedules again.

"I can't believe it," Mandie said with a big smile. "We got our same room back this year, and now we're going to be in classes together."

"It might have been better, Mandie, if we had been in separate classes—" Celia began.

Mandie looked at her sharply and interrupted, "In separate classes? Why—"

"Mandie," Celia interrupted her, "you didn't let me finish. If we were in separate classes, then you could watch the girls in your class and I could watch the girls in my class, and maybe we could catch up with whoever is doing all these terrible things to you."

"I'm sorry, Celia," Mandie said. "You're right about that, but I'd rather be in classes with you anyhow. I'll catch the culprit sooner or later."

The girls for the second sitting were already forming a line in the corridor, and Mandie quickly pulled out her piece of paper to write down the names of the ones she knew.

"Mandie, please hurry," Celia told her. "We

have to go upstairs to get our notebooks before we can go to classes."

Mandie stuffed the paper and pencil back into her pocket and said, "I'm finished."

They hurried to their room and came back downstairs with their notebooks. As they walked toward the room for their first class, Mandie remembered something.

"Go ahead, Celia," Mandie told her. "I'll be there in a minute. I've got to see Miss Prudence."

Celia looked at her in surprise and asked, "See Miss Prudence?"

"Yes, I want to ask her if Uncle Cal is going to check on my grandmother's house today. You go on ahead," said Mandie as she walked down the hallway toward the office.

Celia walked the other way but glanced back at her as she continued on the way to Miss Cameron's class.

Mandie expected to find Miss Prudence in the office, but when she came to the doorway, she couldn't see anyone inside. She tapped lightly on the door facing and called, "Miss Prudence, may I come in for a minute?"

There was no answer, but Mandie thought she heard someone moving about. She took one step into the outer room, and looked around. "Miss Prudence?" she called again.

She couldn't see into the connecting room where Miss Hope had her office, but she knew it was her turn to be at the table in the dining room for the second sitting right now.

Mandie turned to leave and instantly collided with Miss Prudence herself, who was just coming in from the hallway.

"Amanda!" Miss Prudence said with a scowl. "What are you doing in here? I have informed you before that you are not allowed in my office without permission." She stood between Mandie and the doorway. The schoolmistress was not much taller than Mandie, but her deep dark eyes were always intimidating.

"I'm sorry, Miss Prudence," Mandie managed to say. "I . . . I was looking for you."

"You knew I was in the dining room waiting for the rest of the girls to leave," Miss Prudence said. "And just *why* were you looking for me?"

"Miss Prudence, would you please tell me—is Uncle Cal going by my grandmother's house today? I'm beginning to be worried because no one is home there," Mandie said.

"Yes, I have told him to go by there on the way to the depot," the schoolmistress replied. "But there's no reason to worry about your grandmother. She can take care of herself. Now, get along to your class before you're late." Miss Prudence motioned for her to leave the room.

"Thank you, Miss Prudence," Mandie said as she quickly left the office.

During the first break between classes that day, Mandie told Celia what had happened when she visited the office.

"Oh, Mandie, you seem to be at the wrong place at the wrong time everywhere you go," Celia said with a gasp. The girls continued down the hallway to their next lesson.

"I know," Mandie agreed. "And I don't know how I'm going to catch up with Uncle Cal today to see if he has any news."

"I don't think you'd better go looking for him,"

said Celia. He'll come looking for you if he finds anyone at your grandmother's home, I'm sure.''

But when it came time for the noon meal, Mandie still hadn't seen Uncle Cal.

She and Celia met Aunt Phoebe in the upstairs hallway while they were hurrying to leave their books in their room before they went to eat. The old woman was walking toward the stairs as they came up.

Mandie stopped directly in front of her and said, "Aunt Phoebe, have you seen Uncle Cal? Has he been by my grandmother's this morning?"

"I ain't seed him since breakfus' dis mawnin'," Aunt Phoebe said. "I'se in a hurry now, I'll be seein' him later." She quickly stepped around Mandie and hurried down the staircase.

Mandie stood and sighed, but Celia said, "Come on, Mandie. We've got to hurry." They continued on to their room.

"I'm so afraid someone will want to buy the school before I get a chance to talk to my grandmother," said Mandie, tossing her books into a chair.

Celia placed her books on the table and said, "I've got to wash up."

The two girls quickly washed up in the bathroom. As they glanced into the big mirror on the wall, Celia pushed back her auburn curls and Mandie smoothed a stray wisp of blond hair.

"Ready?" Celia asked.

"Ready," Mandie confirmed.

They rushed down the stairs to the dining room and got there just in time. As soon as they had eaten and been dismissed, they raced back to their room to get their books and then hurried on to their next class.

Mandie didn't see Uncle Cal anywhere that day until late in the afternoon. Classes were over and she and Celia were on the front porch with several other girls. The old man came driving up in the rig with Polly Cornwallis and two other new students.

He was unloading luggage while his passengers left the rig when Mandie called, "Uncle Cal!" as she hurried to catch up with him.

Polly noticed Mandie before he had a chance to speak. "Mandie, I finally got here," Polly said.

"You'd better hurry and check into the office, Polly," Mandie told her as she ran down the steps to the rig. She really didn't want to start a conversation with Polly now. She wanted to find out about her grandmother. "Uncle Cal, did you go by my grandmother's?" she asked.

The old man picked up a valise and replied, "Yes, Missy, I dun been by, but still ain't nobody home. I'll be a tryin' agin soon." He looked down at her with a smile before he carried his load of luggage up the stairs and through the front door.

Polly gave Mandie another glance, and then she and the two other new students went inside.

Celia joined Mandie in the yard. "I see your neighbor, Polly, has finally arrived," Celia remarked.

"Yes, and Uncle Cal still hasn't found anyone home at my grandmother's," Mandie replied as she walked around the yard.

"But I heard him say he was going back," Celia reminded her.

When Mandie got in line that night for supper, she was surprised to see Polly Cornwallis also waiting.

"Mandie," Polly called back to her. "I managed to get the same time to eat that you do."

"I see," Mandie replied.

Polly got out of line and came back to stand with Mandie and Celia.

"You know how I did it?" Polly asked. Without waiting for a reply, she said, "I just told Miss Prudence that you and I are dear friends and neighbors when she told all the new girls that one of us needed to go to the first sitting to even things out." She smiled.

"That's fine, Polly," Mandie said. "I hope you're able to wake up and get down here on time in the mornings. You see, we have to be in place by seventhirty."

Polly's smile faded. "Seven-thirty?" she said with a slight moan.

"Yes, seven-thirty—dressed and in line," Mandie repeated.

Polly cleared her throat and said with a reluctant smile, "Well, if you can do it, so can I."

When they entered the dining room, Mandie learned that Polly would be seated at the far end of the table from her. She hoped Polly didn't try to change places in order to be nearer, because Polly would be in for a big surprise when Miss Prudence explained that no talking was allowed during the meal. Mandie decided that was a good rule to have sometimes.

Mandie kept trying to write her list of people, but she realized it was proving to be almost impossible to keep up with everyone. After the girls were dismissed, Polly followed her and Celia out of the dining room and onto the front porch. Mandie couldn't take out her paper and write names on it because Polly would ask what she was doing. So she tried to remember the girls she saw coming and going on the porch.

Mandie decided that she might have been too unfriendly with Polly, so she invited her to walk around the yard. "Come on, Polly," Mandie said. "Celia and I usually walk when we have a chance." Mandie went down the porch steps, and Celia and Polly followed.

"Do you think you're going to like this school?" Celia asked.

"I suppose so," Polly said, shrugging her shoulders.

"Did your kinpeople come with you on the train? I didn't see anyone with you when you got here," Mandie said.

"My aunt Sue and uncle Bert came with me, but when we got to the depot, the driver from the school was waiting with the rig. These other two girls had just come in on another train, so my aunt and uncle went on home because they knew I'd have someone riding with me," Polly explained. "You see, they live a long way out in the country from here, and their driver had their carriage at the depot."

"I don't think I've ever met them," Mandie remarked as they strolled on down the hill.

"No, this is the first time they've visited us since you came to live with your uncle John. They don't travel much because they're old. In fact, they're my mother's aunt and uncle and my great-aunt and great-uncle," Polly said.

"Did you happen to see my mother before you left?" Mandie asked.

"Oh yes, I saw her after you left yesterday, when Joe and Dr. Woodard had come back," Polly said, looking directly at Mandie.

"Joe and Dr. Woodard came back to my mother's house? My mother is not sick I hope," Mandie said anxiously.

"No, she's not sick. He had to come back to visit someone else—a Mrs. Garrett or something—someone I never heard of, and they stayed at your house last night," Polly said.

Mandie wanted to ask if Polly had spent some time with Joe, but she didn't want Polly to think she was jealous. So she asked, "Are they coming on over here to Asheville?"

"No, as far as I know they were going back home to Swain County," Polly said. "Are you expecting them over here?"

Mandie decided she didn't want Polly to know that Joe had promised to come visit. She shrugged and flipped around to smooth a petal on a bright red rose. "Who knows? They may come and they may not," she said.

Suddenly the big bell in the backyard began ringing. Mandie and Celia looked at each other. It wasn't even dark yet, and it was too early for curfew. What was happening? Mandie glanced back up at the schoolhouse and saw the other students rushing into the house.

"Come on," Mandie told Celia and Polly. "Let's see what's going on."

Mandie led the way, and when they caught up with the other girls, they found everyone going into the chapel, which was used for various meetings.

As they looked for seats Mandie noticed Miss Prudence was standing on the platform waiting, and she was holding her little silver bell.

Miss Prudence shook the bell and said loudly, "Young ladies, please be seated. Quickly. This will take only a few minutes."

Mandie saw Miss Hope join Miss Prudence. Miss Hope was taller and much larger than her sister. They were so different in other ways too, and Mandie wondered how they could be sisters.

This must be an important meeting for the two headmistresses to call them together at a special time like this.

Miss Prudence waited until everyone was quiet. When the room became silent, she spoke. "Young ladies, my sister, Miss Hope, and I would like to make a very important announcement." She paused to clear her throat as she glanced at Miss Hope. "As you all have been told, we have put our school up for sale." She paused and looked at her sister again. "We would like to inform you that we have some prospective buyers coming to look at it this weekend." She paused again.

Mandie's heart did flip-flops. *Oh, where is Grandmother?* she wondered. Someone else was about to buy the school.

"Now, in the meantime, we must get prepared to show these people what kind of school we have here," Miss Prudence continued. "Therefore, we are planning on having the students from Mr. Chadwick's School for Boys over for tea on Saturday afternoon. I expect each of you to be on your best behavior and to act like the young ladies you are supposed to be."

A sigh went across the audience, and Miss Prudence quickly tinkled her little bell. When all was silent again, she said, "That is all for now—and please remember what is expected of you. You are dismissed now." She and Miss Hope left the platform.

The students laughed and talked among themselves as they went into the hallway.

Mandie looked at Celia and said, "You know what this means?"

Celia nodded.

"This means what?" Polly asked.

"Oh, just that we're hoping the school won't be sold to someone we don't know," Mandie explained vaguely. "I think I'll go to my room now and write my mother a letter." She walked toward the staircase.

"I need to do that, too," Celia said.

Polly just looked at the two girls and said, "See you later." She went back out the front door to rejoin the other students.

Mandie was going to have to make some quick plans.

Chapter 6 / Help From Tommy

Once back in their room, Mandie took paper and pen from the drawer in the table and sat down to write a letter to her mother. Celia got out her supplies and sat in the other big chair.

"Dear Mother, something terrible is happening," Mandie said quietly to herself as she began to write. "Some strangers are coming here to look us over and decide whether they would like to buy our school. And I have not been able to find Grandmother. She wasn't at home when I got here, and I had to leave Snowball with Aunt Phoebe and Uncle Cal in their house." She paused to think. Glancing at Celia, who was busy writing, she said, "I can't say that. My mother will think something terrible has happened to my grandmother and she will be upset."

Celia looked up and answered, "Sounds like you're telling her that your grandmother is missing or something."

Mandie wadded up the piece of paper. "I was, but I don't want to upset my mother," she said.

"Do what I'm doing," Celia said. "Just write that you arrived all right. We have our old room and our old schedule, and you miss her."

"Yes, I'll just do that," Mandie said. "I do miss her, and I should drop her a few lines. But, Celia, what are we going to do about those people who are coming to look over our school?"

"Mandie, there is nothing we can do," Celia told her. "Your grandmother might be able to do something, but since we can't find her, we're just plain stuck."

"I have an idea," Mandie said, straightening up in her chair. "I could send a note to Tommy Patton and ask him to come over here to talk to us before Saturday."

"And how are you going to get a message to him?" Celia asked.

"That's easy, Uncle Cal will take it for me, I'm sure," Mandie replied. "And I could ask Tommy to bring Robert with him if you'd like."

Celia blushed and said, "We-ell, if you want to." And then she hurriedly asked, "Mandie, just what are you going to talk to Tommy about?"

"About how we can stop Miss Prudence from selling the school until I have an opportunity to ask my grandmother," Mandie explained.

"And suppose your grandmother is not interested and these prospective buyers are really nice?" Celia asked.

"My grandmother is experienced in business, and she can usually work things out," Mandie said as she curled up in the chair. "I have another idea, too. I'll just write a note and ask Uncle Cal to stick it in the door at my grandmother's house. She'll find it as soon as she does come home."

Mandie wrote her notes right away, but she had to wait until the next morning to find Uncle Cal. She gave him the notes and asked him to promise to deliver them.

Later, after the noon meal, she saw him in the front hallway, and he told her that he had left the note on her grandmother's front door and that he had delivered the other message to Tommy.

"And dat felluh, he sent you back a note," Uncle Cal told her as he pulled a folded piece of paper from his pocket and handed it to her, then turned to go down the hallway.

Mandie thanked him and quickly unfolded the paper and read, "Miss Prudence has asked to borrow some more books, and Robert and I volunteered to take them after the evening meal today. Watch for me at the front door. Tommy."

"That was fast!" Mandie exclaimed to herself as she hurried to find Celia and give her the news.

She caught up with Celia on the way to their class and showed her Tommy's note.

"Oh, goodness!" Celia exclaimed. "This is happening so fast. I hope you have something prepared to say to Tommy."

Mandie laughed. She knew Celia was flustered knowing that she would be seeing Robert Rogers that night. And, unlike Mandie, Celia liked to have plenty of time to think things out ahead of time.

"Don't worry," Mandie told her as they entered the classroom. "I'll do all the explaining to Tommy."

Celia brooded over the upcoming visit by the boys until after supper, when she and Mandie were finally able to go out on the front porch and wait.

They didn't have to wait long. The rig from Mr. Chadwick's school came up the driveway, and when it stopped, the two boys jumped down. Mandie noticed that several of the girls on the porch looked their way.

Mandie thought Tommy must have grown a few inches, even though he had already been taller than Joe Woodard, who was the same age. Tommy's dark brown eyes lit up when he saw Mandie. He quickly reached inside the rig for the boxes of books.

Robert gave Celia a shy smile and turned to assist Tommy with the boxes.

"I'm so glad you all could come," Mandie said to them in a low voice so that the other students couldn't hear as the boys carried the boxes through the front door.

Mandie and Celia waited in the alcove near the front door for the boys to take the boxes to Miss Prudence's office. They were back in a few minutes, and Mandie suggested, "Let's walk in the yard so the other girls can't hear what we have to say."

Once they reached the rose garden down the hill, Mandie began to talk about the school. She explained to Tommy about her grandmother not being home and about the prospective buyers coming that weekend. She also told him about the molasses and what had happened to Snowball's sandbox.

"What can we do to keep the buyers from wanting to buy the school?" Mandie asked.

"I'd say you have a problem. But, you know, most problems can be solved," Tommy said with a big smile. "Since Robert and I will be here Saturday for tea, the tea you told me Miss Prudence is planning, we could stage something not very ladylike so that the buyers get the impression that the girls are not being 'taught to act like young ladies,' as Miss Prudence likes to say.''

"Like what?" Mandie asked.

Celia and Robert stood by listening.

"Now don't plan on getting me into trouble too, Tommy," Robert protested.

"Or me," Celia said.

Tommy looked at Mandie and said, "Well, that leaves us."

"Since I'm already on Miss Prudence's bad list, I can't do something worse that would cause her to expel me," Mandie said. "Let's just do something on the borderline, something that would look accidental, maybe."

"Since you girls are supposed to show the buyers, what young ladies you are, maybe you could do something that is unexpected . . ." Tommy cleared his voice as he continued, "like holding hands with me, maybe." He grinned and added, "I'd like that."

Mandie frowned at first and then said, "All right. I'll make it look as though I like it too."

"Mandie, you know we have to wear our white gloves to tea, and Miss Prudence has always forbidden us to even touch one of the boys," Celia reminded her,

"I know," Mandie said. "But I have to take a chance—unless Grandmother comes home before Saturday." She glanced up the hill toward the house and saw Miss Prudence standing on the front porch looking at them. "I think we'd better walk back up to the house. We are being watched."

"And Robert and I have to go back to our school," Tommy added. "Anyway, you can count on me. We'll figure out the details Saturday."

Tommy and Robert bid the girls goodbye and got into the rig. As Tommy drove down the driveway, Mandie and Celia watched. When the girls turned back to go up the steps to the porch, Mandie noticed Miss Prudence had disappeared.

"Mandie, please don't get in trouble. If you get expelled, what good would it do for you to try to save the school from being sold?" Celia asked as they sat in rocking chairs at the far end of the porch.

Before Mandie could answer, she looked up and whispered a warning to Celia, "Here comes Polly. She probably saw us talking to the boys."

As soon as she got within speaking distance, Polly said, "I saw y'all out in the yard with those two good-looking fellows. Where are they from?"

"Oh, Tommy's family are friends of ours. My mother, in fact, went to school right here with his mother and Celia's mother too," Mandie explained, hoping that would satisfy Polly's curiosity.

"I suppose they are from Mr. Chadwick's School for Boys that all the girls are talking about," Polly said as she sat down in a nearby chair. "So they'll be back Saturday for the tea, then."

"That's right," Mandie said. "Lots of other boys, too. Just wait and see."

"Do any of the boys and girls see each other regularly?" Polly asked.

"That is not allowed," Celia told her.

"So then the girls are free to talk to any of the boys?" Polly asked.

"Of course, if you can manage to get one's attention before all the other girls gang up," Mandie said with a laugh.

"The teas Miss Prudence has here with the boys

are formal, Polly," Celia said. "The girls dress up and, of course, the boys do too. They are supposed to act like grown-up society."

"That won't be any problem. My mother has teas sometimes for friends," Polly said as she pushed back her dark hair. "How many boys come to these teas?"

"Oh, lots and lots of boys. You see, there are more boys at Mr. Chadwick's school than there are girls here, so there's a surplus every time," Mandie explained. "Don't worry. You'll be able to meet a lot of them."

About that time, April Snow walked toward them, swinging her long skirts as she held her head aloof. She went on by to sit by herself. Mandie noticed she kept glancing back at them. *She's probably wondering who Polly is*, Mandie thought, *and whether she's a friend of ours.*

"That girl that just went by, I've been seeing her around a lot, but she never seems to mix with the other girls. She's always alone," Polly said.

"She really doesn't have many friends," Celia explained. "I feel sorry for her, but she won't let any of the girls get to know her. Her name is April Snow."

"She doesn't want any friends," Mandie remarked as she remembered times when April had caused her trouble. "And I would advise you not to tangle with her, because she can really stir up trouble."

The three girls talked for a while longer, and then Mandie decided she would go to her room to catch up on some letter-writing.

"I'll be up in a little while," Celia told Mandie.

"I'm in one of those big rooms on the second

floor where there are four beds, so I'm not anxious to go up there until I have to," Polly said.

Mandie was about to leave but remembered something. She said, "That's another thing I overheard Miss Prudence and Miss Hope talking about last year. They were planning to put up partitions to divide the larger rooms into four smaller ones. But they haven't done it, have they?"

"I don't think so," Polly said. "I noticed several other large rooms. You and Celia sure are lucky to have your own private room."

"That room was not being used for students when I came last year, but it seems I was one too many students, and they didn't have anywhere else to put me," Celia explained.

"And then I moved in with her. It took some doing, but we talked Miss Prudence into allowing us to hare the room," Mandie said. "Good-night, Polly. See you in the room, Celia."

When Mandie opened the door to their room and stepped inside, she immediately sensed something was wrong. Then her eyes fell on a stack of papers lying on the table.

"What is that?" she said aloud to herself as she crossed the room to look at the pile of papers. She gasped as she examined the stack. These were some of the students' files. "How did these get in here? Oh no! Someone is making trouble for me again!"

She took slow, deep breaths, trying to calm herself in order to figure out what she should do. "If Miss Prudence finds out these are in here, it will be the end of everything," Mandie cried to herself. "Maybe I can put them back in the office without anyone seeing me."

She stood there a moment thinking about what she should do. Then she quickly removed a pillowcase from one of her pillows and crammed the files inside. After laying the pillowcase on the floor and rolling it up, she picked it up and cautiously opened the door to the hall. There was no one in sight.

Mandie decided to go down the back stairs that led to the kitchen. Maybe she wouldn't meet anyone this way except possibly one of the servants.

She didn't, and once she safely reached the main floor she had to slowly make her way around the back corridors until she got to the office.

When she finally arrived at the office door, she paused to listen. There was no sound. She opened the door, rushed over to Miss Prudence's desk, and quickly removed the files from the pillowcase. One last paper stuck in the bottom of the pillowcase, and she had to roll the sides down in order to reach the paper. She accidentally sideswiped the files she had placed on the desk with the pillowcase, but she quickly caught them just as they were about to spill all over the floor.

"Amanda! What are you doing in my office again?" Miss Prudence demanded from the doorway.

Mandie managed to shake out the last paper and quickly wadded up the pillowcase, holding it behind her. "Oh, Miss Prudence," was all she could say.

Miss Prudence walked to the desk and looked at the files. Mandie could see the anger rising in her face. "Amanda, I will not stand for this. You've been meddling in the student files," the schoolmistress said sharply. She turned to look at Mandie, who was now shaking with fright. "What do you think you've been doing? I've already warned you to stay out of my office, and now I find you in confidential papers. You leave me no choice, Amanda. I will have to take strong disciplinary action."

Mandie tried to talk, but her teeth chattered. "M-M-Miss P-P-Prudence, somebody put those papers in my room. I was only bringing them back," she tried to explain.

"Amanda, you will go to your room right now," Miss Prudence ordered. "My sister and I will decide in the morning what is to be done about this offense. Go!" The old lady motioned toward the doorway.

Mandie realized Miss Prudence was shaking as badly with anger as she was from fright. Mandie ran past the schoolmistress and up the stairs, not stopping until she reached her room. Pushing the door open, she rushed inside and almost knocked Celia down.

"Mandie!" Celia exclaimed as she grabbed the corner of the bureau to keep her balance after the collision.

"Oh, Celia, I'm sorry," Mandie said as she flopped into a chair. "The top just blew off Miss Prudence's anger."

"What? Where have you been?" Celia asked as she sat down nearby.

Mandie explained what had happened. "Somebody stole those papers and put them in here to cause me trouble," she cried. "I just can't figure it out. Why does somebody keep doing things to me when I haven't done anything to anybody else? It doesn't make sense."

"No, it doesn't," Celia agreed. "Mandie, what do you suppose Miss Prudence and Miss Hope will do to you?"

"The worst thing they can think of. They'll probably expel me, and I'll have to go home. My grand-mother is not even here, so I can't go to her house," Mandie moaned. "Celia, I've got to find whoever is doing all these things. But I don't know how to start. Why would anyone steal papers out of the office and bring them in here? Not only that, but why didn't whoever it was get caught in the office?"

"Mandie, tell me honestly," Celia began as she looked at Mandie. "When you left Polly and me on the porch, you didn't go to the office instead of coming up here to our room, did you?"

"Celia!" Mandie shouted at her, and she jumped up and paced around the room. "You don't believe anything I say, do you? I suppose you'll be glad to be rid of me when they expel me from school, too." She threw herself down on the bed and buried her face in the pillow.

Celia ran to her side. "Mandie, please forgive me," she begged. "I didn't mean anything by that. I wanted to ask if you went by the office and saw anyone come out of there?" She touched Mandie's shoulder.

Mandie rolled away from her and said, "Leave me alone, Celia."

Celia slowly rose and sat back down in the chair. A few minutes later, she began getting ready for bed. When Celia was ready to get into bed, Mandie quickly jumped up and plopped into one of the big chairs.

And that's where Mandie spent the night. She didn't even change into her nightclothes. She stayed awake most of the night trying to figure out what was going on.

Early in the morning, Mandie straightened her cramped legs and went to the bathroom to wash her face. Her clothes were crumpled and her hair was tangled, but she didn't care. She had decided during the night she would leave this place and go home. Her mother would just have to allow her to go to the local school in Franklin.

When Mandie returned to the room, Celia was up and getting dressed.

Mandie didn't speak, but turned to go out the door into the hallway. She was going to tell Miss Prudence she was going home. Celia glanced at her but didn't say anything.

As Mandie neared the office downstairs, she could hear Miss Hope and Miss Prudence talking inside. She slowed down to think, to decide what she would say to Miss Prudence. Then it dawned on her that the two ladies were discussing her situation.

"Sister, I know what Amanda has been doing looks bad but, remember, we need a large donation from her grandmother to keep this place running for a while longer. If we send her granddaughter home, there's no way we'll get a cent," Miss Hope said.

"Well, I certainly can't just let her get away with what she has been doing," Miss Prudence said.

"We could make it sound stern, somehow. Maybe we could just say we're going to discuss her behavior with her grandmother and that we'll let her know after that what our decision will be," Miss Hope suggested.

Mandie's heart beat hopefully as she realized the two schoolmistresses weren't going to do a thing to her. *Well, so what,* she thought. It wasn't her fault someone had been doing all those things and making it look like she was involved. Miss Prudence wouldn't believe a thing she said. But the woman wanted her grandmother's money.

"Uh-huh," Mandie said firmly to herself. "I'll just do a little threatening myself." She walked heavily so the women would hear her coming down the hallway, then she stopped in the doorway of the office. The two ladies looked at her in surprise.

"Miss Prudence," Mandie said, clearing her throat, "I've come to tell you that I am withdrawing from your school and will be going home." She watched for reactions from the ladies. The two schoolmistresses looked at each other and then back at Mandie. They seemed surprised.

"What are you saying, Amanda?" Miss Prudence asked, visibly worried.

"I am going home. I have come to tell you I don't want to stay here any longer than it takes me to pack and get a train home," Mandie said.

"Young lady, you are not going anywhere unless a responsible adult comes to get you, and since your grandmother is evidently still out of town, I'd say your mother will have to come before we will allow you to leave," Miss Prudence told her.

Mandie didn't know what to say to that. Her threat had really worked.

"Now go back to your room and get ready for breakfast. You look as though you had slept in that dress," Miss Prudence told her. "We will talk with your grandmother as soon as we can find her. In the meantime, you are not to leave this school. Do you understand?"

Mandie didn't even reply, but quickly turned around and went back upstairs to her room. She realized she would have to eat because she was not allowed to go anywhere. So she went straight to the chifferobe and took down a fresh dress. Celia was dressed and was brushing her hair. She looked at Mandie but didn't speak.

Mandie decided silence was the best route to follow today. She had a lot of thinking to do. But she had already made one decision: when classes broke for lunch, she was going to slip out and go over to her grandmother's house to see for herself whether anyone was home. If she were caught, at least it would be for something she had really done.

Chapter 7 / Visitors

The day dragged for Mandie. She didn't hear much that the teachers said during the morning classes. Celia kept looking at her, concern on her face, but neither spoke. Finally the bell rang for noon break.

"I'm just not going to take the time to carry these books upstairs," Mandie mumbled to herself. She quickly shoved them under a chair in the alcove and hoped no one would find them.

The other girls hurried down the hallways to go up to their rooms and get ready for the noon meal. Mandie slipped out unseen through the front door. She picked up her long skirts and rushed down the driveway to the road. Once on the road, she ran.

Her grandmother didn't live very far from the school. Mandie had walked there several times before. She ran up her grandmother's driveway as she looked about the yard. No one was in sight. Still running, she came to the front door and started to pound on it, but stopped when she realized her note was not on the door where Uncle Cal said he had left it. *There must be someone home,* she thought.

"Grandmother!" Mandie called loudly as she began banging on the front door again.

To her surprise, the door opened, and there stood Annie, Mrs. Taft's upstairs maid. "Missy, whut you doin' heah?" the young girl asked.

"Oh, Annie," Mandie said as she stepped into the front hallway. "Where is my grandmother? I've got to see her." She started down the corridor.

"She ain't heah, Missy," Annie told her.

Mandie stopped and looked at Annie. "But where is she? I've been trying to get in touch with her ever since I checked into the school Monday. I need to talk to her real bad."

"Slow down, Missy," Annie said. "She be back soon as she find dat Hilda."

"Find Hilda? Where is Hilda?" Mandie asked. Hilda was the young girl Mrs. Taft had taken into her home because her parents were unable to raise her.

"Ev'ybody been lookin' fo' dat girl," Annie explained. "She jes' disappeared Sunday. Nowhere to be found. Miz Taft, she got Ben drivin' her all over de countryside lookin' fo' dat girl."

Mandie frowned. She knew Hilda had sometimes roamed off by herself. "But where have you and Ella been? Uncle Cal has been coming by here and couldn't find anyone home," she said.

"Ella, she done gone home fo' a few days," Annie said. "Huh mothuh, she be sick. And Miz Taft, she tells me to he'p out at de church wheah she go. Dey a fixin' to have dat bazah. And I been in and out most days."

"Well, of all things," Mandie said. "If I had just

thought to ask Uncle Cal to leave a note in the door on Monday, you would have gotten it."

"But, Missy, I got de note he left, but I cain't give it to Miz Taft till she come home," Annie said.

"You're right," Mandie agreed with a big sigh. "Annie, do you have any idea when my grandmother might come home? It's real important that I see her as soon as possible."

"No, Missy, she say she come back when she find Hilda," Annie said.

Mandie walked back to the front door and said, "I've got to run back to the school before I'm missed. Annie, please tell my grandmother the minute she walks in the door that it's important— very, very important—that I see her at once."

"Dat I will, Missy," Annie agreed.

Mandie rushed back to school and couldn't believe her good luck—she found she was not late for the meal. The girls were just beginning to file into the dining room. Mandie was the last one in.

Celia turned to look at her when Mandie took her place behind her chair. Mandie felt a pain in her heart as she thought about the disagreement they had had. Maybe things would clear up.

All through the meal Mandie pushed the food around on her plate. She had no appetite. So many things were on her mind. *Where in the world had Hilda gone?* she asked herself. *And why did she run away?* The girl couldn't talk except for a few words, but her grandmother had been able to make the girl happy in her home. Mandie wished she could do something to help in the search.

She thought about her other concerns. There was the problem of the possible sale of the school. And the big problem was finding who was doing things to get her in trouble. She had so much to think about.

Miss Prudence didn't approach Mandie all day about the incident in her office. Having overheard her conversation with Miss Hope, Mandie knew she wouldn't have anything to say about it until she had contacted her grandmother. Even then, Mandie thought the schoolmistress would decide on a light punishment, if any at all, for Mandie having had the files.

Mandie went about in silence the rest of the day. The night passed, and the next morning, which was Friday, held no solutions to her problems. She just wondered when the prospective buyers would actually arrive at the school.

That question was answered after supper that night when she saw an unfamiliar carriage pull up at the doorway of the school. Most of the students were inside somewhere, probably doing homework or writing letters, Mandie suspected. The only ones on the porch were April Snow, who was seated at the far corner, and Etrulia Batson, who was in the swing. Mandie was sitting in a rocker at the opposite end of the long veranda.

The driver of the carriage jumped down and opened the door. Mandie watched as a tall, buxom lady in severely trimmed black clothes descended to the walkway. A man, also in black, followed. Mandie noticed he was not quite as tall as the lady, and he looked about, seemingly at a loss as to what to do next.

"We will just step inside, Attrum," the woman told the man as she led the way to the front door. Attrum still looked about and, when he saw Mandie, halfway smiled at her and quickly disappeared into the schoolhouse, right behind the lady. The driver drove the carriage toward the backyard.

"So that's the buyer!" April Snow said loudly, with an added "humph!" as she rose and went inside the house.

Etrulia looked at Mandie and said, "Me too!" She followed April inside.

"Well, me too!" Mandie said to herself as she also entered the house.

Miss Prudence was in the hallway greeting the strangers. "Do come in," she said. "We're so glad you could visit us today, Mrs. Halibut, Mr. Halibut. If you'll follow me I'll show you the guest room where you can refresh yourselves, and then perhaps we can have a little talk if you are not too tired." She started walking back toward the room reserved for guests near the office.

"Oh, we're not tired at all," Mrs. Halibut replied as she followed Miss Prudence. "We had a pleasant journey."

The two ladies disappeared through the doorway of the guest room, and Mr. Halibut followed slowly.

Mandie went back out onto the front porch, which was deserted now, even though it was not yet dark. She wondered why no one else was outside. That was unusual this early in the evening. Then she had a thought—maybe everyone was avoiding her. Maybe word had gotten around that she was in trouble and no one wanted to be seen with her.

Uncle Cal came up the driveway in the rig. When he got out, Mandie walked over to the steps to speak to him. "I went over to my grandmother's house when classes let out at noon," Mandie told him, "and Annie was home." She explained that her grandmother was looking for Hilda, and that everyone but Annie was gone, but that Annie had been in and out of the house.

"I sho' is glad you found out sumpin', Missy, 'cause I was a gittin' worried myself," the old man replied. He started toward the front door, saying, "Now I'se got work to do."

"Oh, Uncle Cal, did you know the prospective buyers for our school just arrived? A Mr. and Mrs. Halibut, and I'd say she's the one wantin' to buy it," Mandie said.

Uncle Cal looked back at her and said, "No, Missy, I don't believe I knew dat. But right now, I'se got to take some books back to Mr. Chadwick's dat dey sent, 'cause dey be de wrong ones fo' heah."

Mandie quickly stepped between him and the front screen door. "Oh, you are going to Mr. Chadwick's. Uncle Cal, would you please take another note to Tommy Patton for me?" She felt in her pocket and luckily found she was still carrying the piece of paper and pencil to write her list, even though she had decided it was hopeless.

"If'n you hurry and git it made, Missy, I'll take it, but Miz Prudence, she be upset if she find out whut we doin'," he said. "Now I got to git de books."

He went on inside. Mandie sat in a nearby chair and scribbled a quick note to Tommy. "The prospective buyers have just arrived, a Mr. and Mrs. Halibut, and just wait until you see them. She acts dictatorial, and he meekly follows. I'd sure hate to have her in charge of my school. See y'all tomorrow, Mandie."

Uncle Cal came through the screen door with a box of books. Mandie quickly folded the piece of paper and handed it to him.

"Thank you, Uncle Cal, I appreciate it," Mandie said. "I do believe you are the only friend I have left."

"Now, now, Missy, you got dat white cat, and you ain't even been to see him since he moved to our house," Uncle Cal teased her as he slowly descended the steps.

"But you know we're not allowed to visit your house," Mandie replied.

"Not de house, but all right fo' the yard and Phoebe, she got dat white cat out in dat yard now on dat fancy red leash-thing," the old man said as he picked up the reins to drive off.

Mandie didn't even answer. She raced around the house and, sure enough, there was Snowball. He was giving Aunt Phoebe a hard time in a struggle to get loose. She laughed and slid down onto the grass as she picked him up.

Aunt Phoebe let go of the leash as she mumbled, "You'd think de po' cat ain't got no owner. Ain't come to visit all week."

Mandie looked up at the old woman and smiled. "Oh, Aunt Phoebe, I'm sorry," she said. "You know I can't go inside your house because of school rules, but I should have realized you'd be bringing him outside." She hugged the cat tightly and told him, "I do love you, Snowball."

Aunt Phoebe sat on a nearby bench and watched.

Mandie looked up at the old woman and said, "My grandmother is not home yet, but Annie is. I suppose Snowball could go and stay with her if he's too much trouble for y'all."

"Who say dat cat trouble? Ain't me," Aunt Phoebe protested and then, with a big smile, she said, "Why, dat cat, he sleep on our bed at night. Soon as we gits de lamps blowed out, he jump right on top of de kivver."

Mandie laughed and said, "That's because he's used to sleeping on my bed." Snowball curled up in her lap and began purring loudly as he patted her skirt with his paws. Then she suddenly remembered the visitors. "Did you know those people have arrived, those people who want to buy our school? I saw them, and let me tell you, that woman could be a strict boss. You ought to have seen the way she treated her husband when they came in."

Aunt Phoebe looked at her seriously for a moment and then laughed. "Lawsy mercy, Missy, dis heah school ain't been sold yit, and I has a idea it ain't gwine be sold long as you be heah," she said.

"Not if I can prevent it," Mandie said. On sudden impulse she decided to take Aunt Phoebe into her confidence. She leaned toward the woman and said in a low voice, "If I can get hold of my grandmother, that Mrs. Halibut won't have much of a chance, because I want my grandmother to buy the school. That's why I've been so anxious to find her."

Aunt Phoebe looked surprised. "But, Missy, how you knows yo' grandmama gwine buy dis heah school? Dat grandmama o' yours, she got a mind of huh own. You knows dat," she said.

"I know," Mandie agreed. "But if she sees that Mrs. Halibut, I think she might do something. I'm not sure what, but I don't believe she would approve of that lady."

"Heah you goes, all wound up 'bout dat lady, and alls you done is see huh come in. You don't know nothin' 'bout dat woman. You cain't jes' jump to condemning huh. Dat wouldn't be right," Aunt

Phoebe said. "Jes' give de lady a chance. You might like huh. Who knows?"

"Oh, Aunt Phoebe, you don't understand. But then, you haven't seen her yet," Mandie protested. "Just wait. You'll understand what I mean."

"I unnerstand lotsa things, Missy," Aunt Phoebe said with a frown. "I sees and I hears, but I don't talk."

Mandie looked at her in puzzlement and asked, "Now what do you mean by that?"

"I knows you bees in trouble wid Miz Prudence," the old woman said. "And I knows she ain't gwine do nuthin' 'bout it."

Mandie grinned and said, "You must have overheard the same conversation I did between Miss Prudence and Miss Hope. They need a donation from my grandmother for the school."

"Dat be de right idea, Missy, but I hears dis heah 'tween dem ladies las' week 'fo' you git heah," Aunt Phoebe explained. "Yo' grandmama come visit to see whut dey be plannin' to do wid dis heah school. Dey tells huh if dey kin take up 'nuf donations to last till next year, dey won't be sellin' de school right now, but I guesses yo' grandmama don't make no donation, 'cause now dey got dem buyers comin'."

"And they've got buyers coming so my grandmother will give money to stop the sale," Mandie said with a big laugh. "Oh, Aunt Phoebe, we've got it all figured out, haven't we?"

"Maybe," the old woman said, smiling at her.

"Now I have to be sure my grandmother knows about these prospective buyers," Mandie said. "If I can just get in touch with her."

Mandie told Aunt Phoebe what she had found

out about Hilda running away and her grandmother trying to find her.

"Dat Hilda, she sho' be trouble," Aunt Phoebe said. "Yo' grandmama is a good woman to gib dat girl a home."

"I know," Mandie agreed. "But then Hilda's parents didn't want her because she can't talk, and they're too poor to give her the medical attention that my grandmother can get for her. I hope my grandmother finds her real soon, and I hope nothing's happened to her."

It had grown dark while they talked, and Mandie knew she would have to go up to her room to get ready for bed before the bell in the backyard began ringing curfew. She rose, set Snowball down, and handed Aunt Phoebe the end of his leash.

"Thanks, Aunt Phoebe, for everything," she said. "I have to go now. See you in the morning."

The old woman waved to her as Mandie ran around the house to enter the front door.

There was no sign of anyone as Mandie ran up the steps and through the door. The hallway was empty, and she hurried up the stairs. She felt a little better now that she had talked to Aunt Phoebe and played with Snowball. The tiff with Celia worried her, and she planned to set things right as soon as she could get to their room.

She was thinking of words to say to Celia as she pushed open the door, but when she looked around the room, it was empty. *Where was Celia?* she wondered. *Oh well, Celia will probably show up by the time I'm ready for bed.*

Mandie put on her nightclothes, picked up a book to read, and crawled into bed to prop up on her pillows. But she couldn't get her mind on the book. By this time tomorrow, she would probably know whether the school had been sold to Mrs. Halibut.

She thought of the scene she and Tommy had planned and smiled to herself. She could imagine the expression on Mrs. Halibut's face when she saw them. And then, with a frown, she thought of what Miss Prudence would do.

"Oh, Grandmother, please hurry and come home," she murmured to herself. "You could change everything."

Mandie felt so tired and worn out. It had been a long week, and tomorrow would be the climax.

Then she thought about Hilda. "Poor Hilda. I do hope she's safe," Mandie said to herself.

Her mind went back to Tommy Patton, who was coming to tea tomorrow. Her eyes grew heavy, but she roused herself to look around the room. "Where is Celia? It must be time for the bell to ring," she said to herself.

She lay back on her pillows and planned what she would say to Celia when she finally came back to their room.

But by the time Celia did come back, Mandie was fast asleep, and the curfew had not even been rung.

Chapter 8 / Teatime

Mandie was awake by dawn the next morning. When she realized it was Saturday, the day of the tea for the prospective buyers, she jumped out of bed to get dressed. She glanced at Celia and saw that she was already awake and looking at her.

"Good morning," Mandie said hesitantly. She waited to see her friend's reaction.

Celia threw back the covers and bounced to her feet. "Good morning," Celia replied as she walked over to the chifferobe to take down a dress.

Mandie followed her, reached for Celia's hand, and looked straight into her friend's eyes. "I'm sorry for being so mean," Mandie told her.

"And I'm sorry for not understanding," Celia said as the two girls embraced.

Mandie pulled back and said, "It's Saturday, and we have a big day ahead of us, remember?"

"Yes, that's right," Celia agreed. She pulled down a dress and said, "I saw the man and woman who came in last night while I was in the library downstairs. I suppose they must be the prospective buyers." She stepped out of her nightclothes and pulled the dress over her head.

"Definitely," Mandie said as she put on her shoes and buttoned them. "I was on the front porch when they arrived. Their name is Halibut, Mr. and Mrs. Attrum Halibut. She's the boss, and he just follows along."

"She looked to me like she could 'out-stern' Miss Prudence," Celia remarked as she brushed her long auburn curls.

"Right," Mandie said as she joined Celia in front of the floor-length mirror standing in the corner. "I'm still hoping my grandmother will come home in time for me to talk to her." Mandie suddenly realized Celia didn't know what she had been doing. She explained how she had slipped out to go to her grandmother's house the day before. She also told Celia what Annie had said about her grandmother and Hilda.

"Hilda," Celia repeated. "Remember when we found Hilda?"

"I sure do," Mandie said, retying the ribbon sash around her blue dress. "Her mother and father had kept her shut up in a room because she doesn't know how to talk. I'm glad we could help her. And, you know, I believe my grandmother has come to really love her."

"Your grandmother is a good person," Celia said.

"Ready to go downstairs?" Mandie asked.

"I suppose we have to, and since Miss Prudence sits with us, I imagine the buyers will eat with us too," Celia said.

"Will you help me watch out for Uncle Cal?" Mandie asked as they left their room and walked down the hallway. "I want to ask him if he will check on my grandmother before we have that tea."

"Of course, Mandie, but Uncle Cal will probably be awfully busy with the strangers here and the boys coming over from Mr. Chadwick's," Celia said as they descended the stairs.

"I know, but maybe he'll have to go in that direction for something else and can stop by her house," Mandie said.

Even though it was Saturday and most of the girls liked to sleep late and make a last-minute dash for the dining room, Mandie noticed that almost everyone was already in line. Polly was standing at the end of the line, which meant that Mandie and Celia would be able to talk to her before they went into the dining room.

"Have you heard what's going on?" Polly quickly asked Mandie and Celia. "Oh, this is going to be an exciting day!"

"What, Polly?" Mandie asked. "I know the prospective buyers are here. I saw them last night, but what else is going on?"

Polly bent closer and whispered, "Most of the girls are talking about staging a rebellion when Miss Prudence introduces the man and woman."

"A rebellion!" Mandie asked in surprise. "Not in the dining room I hope, or we may not be able to eat."

"Oh no, they're planning some show of protest against these people," Polly continued in a whisper. "Have you seen them? That woman could really be a strict schoolmistress."

"Do you not know what the girls are talking

about doing?" Celia asked.

"It will be at the tea—if they do anything," Polly said. "They haven't made any definite plans yet, but April Snow says they will decide before tea-time."

"April Snow?" Mandie and Celia both asked.

Polly nodded, and Mandie said, "If April Snow told you this, I don't think I'd believe a word of it. In the first place, none of the other girls would go along with her because they know she causes so much trouble. And I'm afraid April makes things up some-times."

"Oh, but I saw her talking to Etrulia Batson. I overheard enough to know Etrulia was going right along with her about the fact that no one seemed to like the looks of the buyers. She said if all of us got together, we could probably influence Miss Prudence's decision or change the buyer's mind," Polly explained.

Mandie and Celia looked at each other in sur-prise.

"Thanks for telling us about this, Polly," Mandie said. "If you hear what they are planning to do, will you let us know?"

"Of course, Mandie," Polly said. "I'm sure you'll want to join in whatever happens."

The line moved on into the dining room, and the girls went to stand behind their chairs. Miss Pru-dence was not in her place, but she rushed in after all the girls were ready, then Millie closed the door to the hallway.

"Evidently the strangers are not eating with us," Mandie whispered to Celia.

Celia nodded agreement.

Miss Prudence tinkled her little silver bell and

said, "Young ladies, before we begin, I want to make
a statement." She looked around the table. "Now
listen closely to what I have to say. We have visitors
here to look at the school in regard to buying it. I
am demanding that each and every one of you put
forth your very best behavior. Anyone breaking our
rules will automatically be expelled and will never
be reinstated for any reason whatsoever. Do you
understand me? Please answer me." She watched
the students closely.

"Yes, ma'am," the students chorused through-
out the room.

"Now you cannot say later that you did not have
proper warning," Miss Prudence told them. "And
your parents will have no recourse but to take you
home. Is that understood?"

"Yes, ma'am," echoed around the table again.

"We will return thanks now and have our meal,"
the schoolmistress said as she watched to see that
every head bowed. "We thank you, dear God, for
this food we are about to receive. Amen. You all
may be seated now."

The students slid into their chairs and glanced
at one another. Mandie decided that someone must
have told Miss Prudence about the girls' plans. That
was too bad, because she would be the only student
breaking the rules when she and Tommy staged
their scene. Mandie wondered if Miss Prudence
would expel her, even though the school needed her
grandmother's money so badly. She hoped her
grandmother would get home so she could talk to
her before the tea.

Mandie looked around the table and caught
glimpses of expressions between some of the girls.
Most of them weren't eating, but were only moving

the food around on their plates. Maybe they were just going to ignore Miss Prudence's warning. After all, if all of the girls violated the rules, Miss Prudence couldn't expel the whole school.

As soon as they were dismissed, the students hurried out the front door. But instead of sitting on the porch, which was the custom, they began walking around the yard together. Polly and April Snow were among them.

Mandie and Celia sat in rocking chairs on the porch and watched the others.

"I have an idea they don't like what Miss Prudence had to say and, not only that, they are probably trying to find out how Miss Prudence found out about their plans," Mandie said in a low voice.

"Do you think they might do something anyway?" Celia asked.

"I'm not sure, but I know Polly won't miss a word, and she said she'd let us know," Mandie said.

"You know, Mandie, I was just thinking. You and I have never exactly mixed with the other girls. I know we're friendly with all of them, and they are with us, but we more or less keep to ourselves."

Mandie laughed and said, "That's because they aren't as adventurous as we are. We're always busy with a mystery of some kind. But I do consider all of them friends."

"I agree. We don't have a whole lot of time for our own at this school," Celia said. "We always have so much homework, there's not much else we can do."

"I would imagine the other girls get together in their rooms and talk, since they all share a room with seven other girls, and we're the only ones alone," Mandie said. "But I don't see how they ever get any homework done."

Polly came up the walkway and sat down in a nearby chair. "The girls are debating whether to go ahead with their plans or not," Polly reported in a low voice. "A few of them are afraid of what their parents would do to them if they were expelled. As for myself, I'm ready to join in on anything they want to do."

"If the girls do show their dislike for the buyers, they should remember that if these people really do buy the school, they're going to have to abide by their rules if they want to stay here," Celia said. "And I would imagine the discipline would be much stricter."

Polly shrugged and said, "I know, but my mother would transfer me to another school if I didn't like the new owners."

Mandie realized this was the truth. She knew Mrs. Cornwallis' daughter could do no wrong and always got her way.

The day moved on. The students went about their usual activities: homework, writing letters, and visiting with each other. Mandie and Celia had to catch up with their personal chores in their room. Now and then Mandie roamed the halls looking for Uncle Cal, and it was almost time for the noon meal when she finally caught up with him.

"Uncle Cal!" Mandie called to the old man as she saw him going down the hallway toward the kitchen.

He stopped and looked back at her. "Yes, Missy," he said.

"I know you're awfully busy today, and I'm not asking any special favors, but if you happen to pass my grandmother's house today on one of your errands, could you please check to see if she has come home?" Mandie asked as she caught up with him.

"Dat I will, Missy," he replied. "I be gwine dat way aftuh we eat now to git mo' s'pplies fo' de tea pahty. I let you know. I promise."

"Thanks, Uncle Cal," Mandie answered as he continued on his way through the door to the kitchen.

"Thank goodness I finally found him," Mandie said to herself as she went back down the hallway.

She went to her room, where Celia was already getting freshened up for the noon meal.

When she entered, Celia was brushing her hair and warned her, "Mandie, you'd better hurry. It's almost time for the bell."

Mandie rushed to the bathroom, washed her face and hands, and came back to brush her hair. She told Celia that she had finally found Uncle Cal, and that he would check on her grandmother. "And I do hope she has come home," she added.

"But, Mandie, even if your grandmother has come home, it will be so near time for the tea, what can you do?" Celia asked.

"If she is home, I'll just run over there and talk to her right fast," Mandie said. "I can do that and get back in time for the tea. With all the fuss going on getting prepared for the occasion, I don't think anyone will even miss me."

"One day you're going to get into bad trouble for cutting corners so close. You'll get delayed, and someone will find out what you're doing," Celia warned her.

"Don't worry about me, Celia," Mandie told her.

When the girls went into the dining room for the

noon meal, they found Mr. and Mrs. Halibut waiting with Miss Prudence.

"Guess we're stuck with them this time," Mandie muttered to Celia as they went to stand behind their chairs.

Miss Prudence tinkled her little silver bell and introduced the guests. "Young ladies, we have guests today, Mr. and Mrs. Halibut," she said, looking around the room. "Would you please welcome them?"

All the students looked at one another in surprise. *What are we supposed to do now?* Mandie thought.

But Celia understood right away. "Welcome to our school," she said, then all the other girls immediately echoed her greeting.

Mr. and Mrs. Halibut nodded in reply, and Miss Prudence once more tinkled her little silver bell. "We will now return thanks," she said.

Mandie noticed the schoolmistress's blessing was more elaborate than usual. When they were all seated, Miss Prudence paid little attention to the girls, but kept up a steady conversation in low tones with the guests.

Finally the meal was over, and Mandie and Celia rushed out onto the front porch to watch for Uncle Cal. Most of the other students went to their rooms, but Polly came outside to join them.

"What's the latest news?" Mandie asked.

"They are all afraid to start something," Polly said. "But if anyone does begin a protest, then all the other girls will back them up."

"But what kind of protest, Polly?" Celia asked.

"Oh, you know, Miss Prudence is going to make the announcement at teatime that the Halibuts are interested in buying the school, which we already know," Polly explained. "She told us this morning at breakfast that these visitors are interested in buying the school. So the girls think the best thing to do would be to wait until Miss Prudence announces this when the Halibuts are present. She will expect us to smile and beam our approval. However, we plan to frown and moan in protest."

Mandie caught her breath. "That's awfully bold, Polly. And it'll be embarrassing to the Halibuts and Miss Prudence and Miss Hope. Couldn't the girls just protest against the sale of the school, and not particularly against the Halibuts? It would amount to the same thing, but wouldn't be as bad."

Polly shook her head. "The girls have been discussing that, but they think it would be better to just bring it all out into the open and let everyone know we don't want the Halibuts to buy our school," she said.

"Oh me," Celia said with a sigh. She turned to Mandie and said, "I think your way would be much better, Mandie. If you could only talk to your grandmother!"

Mandie nodded in agreement. "I just have to wait and see if Uncle Cal gets back in time for me to"—she looked at Polly and doubted she could trust her not to say anything about her plan—"follow through."

"What does your grandmother have to do with this?" Polly asked as she watched Mandie closely.

"Who knows?" Mandie said. "It might be a whole lot, but then again nothing."

"Mandie, tell me, are you planning something?" Polly asked, eagerly leaning forward.

Mandie thought for a moment and then said,

"Polly, what I am trying to do has to be kept a secret for the time being, but I promise I will let you know as soon as I can if I'm successful."

Before Polly could reply, Mandie looked up and saw Uncle Cal coming up the driveway in the rig. But instead of driving to the front door, he detoured into the backyard. Mandie quickly stood up and said, "Excuse me, I'll be right back." She gave Celia a knowing look.

Polly looked from one to the other and said, "I have to go now." She stood up also.

"But, Polly, Mandie will be right back. Tell me more about the girls' plans," Celia said as Mandie rushed through the front door to look for Uncle Cal.

Mandie heard Polly say, "Well, I'll wait a few minutes if she's coming right back."

Mandie was able to get through to the backdoor without being seen. She opened the outside door and looked out. Uncle Cal had supplies on the rig and was beginning to unload them.

"Uncle Cal," Mandie called to him as she stepped into the yard. "Any luck?"

The old man shook his head. "No, Missy, yo' grandmama ain't home yit, but Annie, she did say she hear Miz Taft be back tomorrow night. And I kin go den if Missy want." He set one of the boxes on the ground.

"Oh yes, please go tomorrow night. I'll see you before then. Thank you, Uncle Cal," Mandie called as she turned and went back into the house.

Tomorrow night? Mandie wondered. *Would Miss Prudence sign an agreement with the Halibuts before then?* She hoped not.

When Mandie returned to the front porch, Polly had gone back into the front yard to talk with the other students. Mandie was glad, because now she could talk to Celia without Polly listening. She wasn't sure if Polly would repeat things to the other girls.

When Mandie told Celia the news that her grandmother might finally be home the next night, Celia asked, "But how are you going to talk to your grandmother?"

"I plan on getting Uncle Cal to find out for sure that she's home, then I will just slip out and go over to her house," Mandie explained.

"Wouldn't it be better for him to ask your grandmother to come over here and talk to you?" Celia asked.

"No, because Miss Prudence would have to know she was here, and I might not even get a chance to talk privately with her," Mandie replied.

Suddenly the bell in the backyard rang, and the girls all knew it was their signal to go to their rooms to get ready for the tea. It would ring again when it was time to come downstairs for the social.

Mandie and Celia avoided the crowd. They waited until the other girls had rushed up the stairs to their rooms, and then they went to theirs.

Mandie wasn't in the mood to get all dressed up, but she knew Tommy Patton would be there. She wanted to look her best for him. She put on one of the new dresses Aunt Lou had made—a pale blue voile trimmed with pink rosebuds made from satin ribbon scattered around the neckline and down the front of the full skirt. She unplaited her long hair, brushed it out, and tied it back with a matching bow. She hung her locket around her neck.

Celia's favorite color was green, and she dressed in a bright green batiste dress trimmed with light cream-colored lace. She put a matching band of green cloth around her head, tied it in a knot, and let the ends hang down on her shoulder.

Both girls had new patent leather shoes, which they wore with white silk stockings. Then they put on their little white gloves that Miss Prudence insisted they wear for such an occasion.

As soon as they were finished dressing, the bell rang again and they went back downstairs. Miss Prudence was in the front hallway directing the girls to various places to sit. The tea table had been set up in the alcove, and the entire hallway and front porch were to be used as the girls found seats.

Mandie saw Polly and asked softly, "Anything going on?"

Polly shrugged her shoulders and said, "I'm not sure." Before Polly could say any more, Miss Prudence motioned Mandie and Celia out onto the front porch and Polly into the parlor.

As they went out the front door, Mandie glimpsed the Halibuts sitting in the alcove, from where they could view the front porch and yard as well as the main hallway and the parlor. Miss Prudence really had everything planned for the strangers to see and hear almost everything that went on.

Mandie and Celia sat in rockers near the corner, and other girls filled up the seats on the porch.

"My, don't we all look lovely?" Mandie said with a giggle as she surveyed the students. "These things make me so uncomfortable. When I'm grown and have a house of my own I'll never have a tea."

Celia laughed and said, "You'll change your mind by then."

The girls looked up and saw several rigs making

their way up the long driveway from the road. The first two belonged to Mr. Chadwick. Uncle Cal followed along behind with the surrey belonging to the girls' school.

"There are so many boys, it takes a lot of rigs to bring them over, doesn't it?" Celia remarked.

"Well, I'm glad there are more boys at that school than there are girls here at our school. That way we don't ever come up short for partners for these fancy doings," Mandie replied with a laugh. "I think I see Tommy there in the first rig." She shaded her eyes with her gloved hand to see the vehicle better.

"And Robert," Celia added as she, too, watched.

Suddenly, something ran across the driveway right in front of the horse pulling the first rig and caused it to stop quickly.

Mandie's heart beat wildly. What was that? She stood up to get a better view as Tommy Patton jumped down from the rig to soothe the horse.

"Snowball!" Mandie cried. She lifted her long skirt and ran into the yard while everyone watched.

"Snowball!" she called out to him. He was busily trying to wash himself under a rose bush. She reached down and grabbed him, and then realized he was covered with black soot. "Oh, Snowball, what have you been into?"

Tommy hurried to her side. "He looks like he's been in something awfully dirty," he said.

At that moment, Aunt Phoebe came hurrying across the yard. "Dat cat," she told them as she reached for Snowball. "He try to git out and fus' thing I knows, he disappear up de chimney. Guess he musta gone clean out on de roof." She put her apron around the cat and took him away.

By this time, Miss Prudence had appeared on the front steps to see what was going on. The boys had all alighted from the vehicles and stood by watching.

"Young men, to the house," Mr. Chadwick told his students, and the boys moved onto the porch.

Mandie stood there in the yard, looking at her dirty gloves and the slight smudge of black on her new dress.

Tommy watched her and then laughed. "Just take off those gloves and you'll look fine," he said.

Mandie quickly rolled the dirty gloves off as she saw Miss Prudence motion to her. She slowly made her way to the front porch and the waiting school-mistress. Tommy followed.

"Amanda, go to your room at once and clean up, and then get back down here promptly," Miss Prudence said sternly as she looked over Mandie's dress. "We will deal with this later."

"Yes, Miss Prudence. I'm sorry, Miss Prudence," Mandie said, meekly walking through the front door. Tommy followed her inside and whispered, "Good start to entertaining your guests!"

"Tommy, this is really embarrassing," Mandie said as she continued toward the staircase. She felt as if everyone were looking at her.

"Hurry upstairs and back. I'll be waiting so we can stage our scene," Tommy said in a low voice.

Mandie knew what he was talking about. But with this happening to the cat, she wasn't so sure she could go through with her plans. "Oh, Snowball, you are always causing trouble!" Mandie moaned as she surveyed herself in the full-length mirror in her room. She cleaned up and worried about what would happen now. She was sure Miss Prudence was angry, and she was sure the Halibuts had seen the whole mess through the window in the alcove.

She had no idea what the schoolmistress might do, and she was afraid to even think about it.

Chapter 9 / Sad News

Fortunately, Mandie was able to remove the smudge from her dress with a soft towel after she washed her hands. She smoothed her hair and straightened her long skirts, and after she put on a clean pair of white gloves, she returned downstairs.

As Mandie slowly descended the long staircase, her eyes darted this way and that to see if Miss Prudence was watching. But she didn't see the schoolmistress until she passed the alcove and saw her conversing with the Halibuts. She hurried on by to the front screen door, where she found Tommy waiting for her.

"Celia and Robert have saved us seats. Come on, this way," Tommy said, motioning toward the far corner of the porch. The tall young man leaned over to whisper, "Hold your chin up. You look even better than you did when you went upstairs." He gave her a big grin.

Mandie smiled up at him and straightened her

shoulders. "Thanks," she whispered back.

"Thank goodness you got back before they served tea," Celia said, lowering her voice as Tommy and Mandie sat down. "Remember, I don't like tea. I hope somebody will come to my rescue and drink mine."

Robert laughed and said, "I believe I drank your tea last time without Miss Prudence ever finding out. I'll try again."

Celia smiled at him.

"I saw Miss Prudence with the Halibuts just now," Mandie said. "I suppose as soon as Mr. Chadwick joins them, the maids will begin serving tea."

At that moment, Millie and a maid from the boys school began moving among the students with a tea tray. Mandie glanced at the door to see Miss Prudence, Mr. Chadwick, and Mr. and Mrs. Halibut coming out onto the front porch.

All the students carefully accepted the cups of tea and sweet biscuits as the adults observed. This was a test of their social decorum, which was an important part of their schooling. Everyone must know how to serve as well as how to balance a teacup and "how to put on airs," as Mandie called it.

Celia held on to her cup and saucer and nervously watched Miss Prudence. Robert quickly drank his tea, and in a split second when the schoolmistress was looking the other way, he switched cups with Celia and consumed her tea.

"Thanks," Celia muttered under her breath.

"Anything for you," Robert replied in a low voice.

Mandie had been watching. She looked at Tommy and said, "You don't have to drink mine. I don't really like tea, but I can manage to drink one cupful. I don't know why we can't just have coffee. After all, we are allowed to choose in the dining room."

Tommy laughed and said, "I suppose you'd say it's not socially acceptable to practice having tea while drinking coffee."

Mandie, Celia, and Robert all laughed. Then suddenly the tinkle of Miss Prudence's little silver bell silenced everyone on the porch.

"Young ladies and young gentlemen, we will now assemble in the front hallway," Miss Prudence announced loudly as she, Mr. Chadwick, and the Halibuts entered the front door.

All the students looked at one another. Mandie knew the other students were deciding whether or not to make their displeasure known when Miss Prudence made the expected announcement about the Halibuts' interest in buying the school. As she and her friends followed the crowd inside, she looked up at Tommy. He winked at her and whispered, "Get ready."

Mandie felt a sudden wave of guilt. She couldn't go through with the scene she and Tommy had planned. For some reason she could hear Uncle Ned reprimanding her for doing such a thing. He wouldn't approve at all. He was her father's friend, and since she had lost her father the year before, she had come to love the old Cherokee Indian.

The little silver bell tinkled again. "Young ladies," Miss Prudence called out. Mandie looked up and saw her, Mr. Chadwick, and the Halibuts standing on the stairway in front of the assembled students. "Since we don't have space available to accommodate all the students of both schools at once, we will stand right here for a short announcement." She paused and looked over the crowd.

Mandie also glanced around the crowd. She tried to judge whether the other girls were going to protest against the Halibuts buying the school or not. She found herself hoping they wouldn't, because it would embarrass the schoolmistresses and their guests. She still believed that her grandmother would buy the school or come up with some solution.

Miss Prudence tinkled her little silver bell again, even though all the students were completely silent. "All you girls from my school have met Mr. and Mrs. Halibut at mealtime in the dining room, and now I will explain why they are visiting us." She paused again and looked over the crowd.

Mandie held her breath and watched. Tommy, smiling, stooped to whisper in her ear, "Don't forget to give me a clue when you're ready for me to hold your hand."

Mandie shook her head to say no, and Tommy looked puzzled.

As she watched for any sign of disrespect from the girls, Miss Prudence continued. "Mr. and Mrs. Halibut are visiting us in order to meet you all and to have a look at our school. As you and your parents have all been told, my sister, Miss Hope, and I have decided to sell the school and retire." Not a single girl moved or spoke, but they all stared at the schoolmistress.

Mandie happened to see Polly nearby, and when Polly looked her way, Mandie mouthed the word, "Now?" Polly shook her head, and her lips formed the word, "No." Mandie thought she meant the girls were not going to protest and blew out a sigh of relief as she turned back to look at Miss Prudence.

Tommy had watched the two girls pass the message and whispered in Mandie's ear, "Now?"

"Changed my mind," Mandie quickly whispered back as she continued to watch Miss Prudence.

"Mrs. Halibut has been a teacher since she was young, and now she would like to retire from the teaching profession and run a school such as ours," Miss Prudence continued. "Mr. Halibut's career is also teaching, and Mr. Chadwick is interested in talking to him about becoming an assistant."

The boys looked at one another with concern when they heard this.

Mandie glanced up at Tommy and noticed he was frowning. No one had known about this.

Miss Prudence continued, "This concludes my announcement about the sale of our school, but I have very grave news to tell you. I received a message last night, but I didn't want to spoil our tea."

Mandie held her breath and waited to hear what this was all about.

"I know of no way to put this except to be straightforward and to the point," Miss Prudence said, clearing her throat. "President McKinley was shot yesterday while attending the Pan-American Exposition in Buffalo, New York."

There was a loud commotion among the students, and Mandie heard herself screaming to be heard, "Oh no, it can't be." Tears blinded her eyes, and Tommy put his arm around her shoulders.

Miss Prudence, with a compassionate look toward Mandie, tinkled her little silver bell to try to restore order. "Yes, Amanda," she said, "I know you visited him last March, and I am sorry to be the one to break the news to you. The report today is that he is holding his own, so there is a possibility of recovery."

The mood of the students turned from confusion to stunned silence. Some of the girls were crying. Some of the boys looked as though they were about to break into tears.

"I will keep you informed when I receive further news," Miss Prudence told them. "You are dismissed now. Our tea is over. Girls, you may talk with your friends until Mr. Chadwick takes his students back to their school."

Mandie couldn't stop crying. Tommy led her out the front door and into the yard. Celia and Robert followed, and they found a bench to sit on.

"Oh, Mandie," Celia said through her tears. She reached out to hold Mandie's hand.

"Miss Prudence did say he seemed to be holding his own," Robert reminded everyone.

"I wonder what happened," Tommy said. And then he added, "Now I know why Mr. Chadwick took the morning newspaper to his office and didn't pass it around to the students as he usually does."

"I was thinking the same thing," Robert said. "And if we could find today's newspaper, we could learn the details." He looked at Celia.

"Miss Prudence must have it hidden away somewhere, because I haven't seen one today," Celia told him. She looked at Mandie.

Mandie's white gloves had become wet from her tears, so she took them off. Tommy gave her his handkerchief. She looked at Celia and said in a quavery voice, "We need . . . to say . . . our verse, because I'm afraid for the President . . . afraid he might die." Her voice broke.

Celia looked at the two boys and explained, "I

don't remember whether y'all have ever been with us when we said it or not, but there's a special verse we say when we're afraid or scared that something bad might happen."

Both boys nodded, and the four young people joined hands while the girls quoted the Bible verse, "What time I am afraid I will put my trust in Thee."

Mandie sniffed and tried to dry her face with Tommy's handkerchief, which was also wet. "Now we just have to trust that the President will get well," she said. Her friends agreed.

The four friends sat and talked until Mr. Chadwick called his students together to return to their school.

"I'm glad we didn't do what we had planned," Mandie told Tommy as he stood on the porch steps.

"I know. I am too," he said with a big smile. "See you soon."

Most of the girls went to their rooms after the boys left. Mandie and Celia went upstairs to their room, changed their dresses, and freshened up to be ready for supper.

As they were changing, Mandie said, "Oh, Celia, I can't imagine who would do such a thing to President McKinley." Her voice was shaking as she spoke. She buttoned her dress and continued, "He's such a nice, friendly man."

"Whoever did it must not be just right in their mind," Celia said.

"I want to know what happened," Mandie said.

———

And after supper she did find out what happened. Miss Prudence informed the girls at the dining table that since there was only one copy of the newspaper she would read aloud the article about the President for any who would like to hear.

Most of the girls followed the schoolmistress into a classroom where she read the account. Mandie learned that a man thought to be mentally deranged had committed this crime, and he was now under arrest. The man had wrapped up his right hand in a bandage and put his arm in a sling. He had gone to the exposition and stood in line to shake hands with the President. But when he came to President McKinley, he reached out his left hand to shake the President's hand and shot the President with a pistol concealed in the bandage around his right hand.

After Miss Prudence had finished and the other girls had left the room, Mandie and Celia sat alone a few moments. Mandie could still see the big, friendly man welcoming her and her grandmother to the White House.

"Please, dear God, let him get well," Mandie prayed softly.

"Yes, please do," Celia added.

They went to their room for the night. As they undressed for bed, Mandie's mind roamed. She wished she could see her grandmother now, so she could talk to her about the President. And she wished she could talk to Uncle Ned, also. He was a friend of President McKinley's. Joe had gone to the White House, as well as Sallie, Uncle Ned's granddaughter.

Celia tried to change the subject. "Mandie, you know, I'm glad the other girls didn't protest when Miss Prudence made the announcement about the Halibuts."

"I am too," Mandie said. "Anyway, it's not even sure that the Halibuts want to buy the school. Evidently they are still looking." She curled up in one of the big chairs.

"I wonder when they will be leaving here," Celia said as she curled up in the other big chair.

"Probably tomorrow," Mandie said. "Do you suppose they'll be going to Mr. Chadwick's school to look it over? Miss Prudence *did* say Mr. Chadwick was interested in Mr. Halibut as an assistant."

"Unless they've already been over there," Celia said.

"But Tommy and Robert didn't know anything about Mr. Chadwick's possible offer of a job, so I don't imagine the Halibuts have been to his school," Mandie said. She got up and walked around the room. "I'll be so glad when tomorrow night comes and I can go over to see my grandmother."

"Was it definite that she would return home tomorrow night?" Celia asked.

"That's what Uncle Cal said, that Annie expected her home tomorrow night," Mandie said, plopping down into the chair again. "He said he would check again tomorrow and let me know if she does come home."

A soft knock sounded on the door, and the two girls looked at each other. It was almost time for the bell in the backyard to ring curfew. Mandie wondered who could be visiting them that late as she rose to answer the door.

Before Mandie could reach it, the door opened slowly, and Aunt Phoebe stuck her head inside.

"Come in, Aunt Phoebe," Mandie told her as the old woman stepped inside.

"I can't stay. Got things to do," the woman said as she looked at Mandie. "I heerd de news 'bout de

President, and I knows how much you think o' him, Missy. I jes' want to be sho' you all right now."

Mandie burst into tears, and Aunt Phoebe reached to take her in her arms. "Now, now," the old woman said, patting Mandie's long blond hair. "I didn't mean to cause all dis. Heah, let's jes' sit down a minute." She led Mandie to the side of the bed, where they sat down together. Mandie leaned her head on Aunt Phoebe's shoulder, and the old woman put her arm around Mandie.

"Oh, Aunt Phoebe, I'm so glad you came to see me. I can't find my grandmother, and my mother and Uncle John are all the way back home, and I don't even know where Uncle Ned is right now, and I didn't have anyone to talk to, except Celia, and she's upset, too," Mandie said in one long, trembling breath.

Celia sat with them on the side of the bed, and Aunt Phoebe embraced Celia with her other arm."

"We jes' hafta remember, it be de Lawd's will de President will git well, but de Lawd don't always git His way down heah," Aunt Phoebe said softly. "And we must 'member to pray fo' him."

"Yes, Aunt Phoebe, we'll do that right now," Mandie said, straightening up to look at the old woman. She reached with one hand for Aunt Phoebe's work-hardened hand, and for Celia's hand with the other. "Aunt Phoebe, you know Uncle Ned always prays with me, but he's not here, so I need you to."

Aunt Phoebe tightened her grip on Mandie's hand, looked upward, and said, "Dear Lawd, heah our prayer. We pray fo' de President to git well. We pray fo' you to lay yo' hands on him and make him well. We love him, O Lawd, and our country need him, 'cause he be a good man. And his sick wife, she need him, too. Send us news, O Lawd, good news, we hopes. We puts all our trust in you.''

"Oh yes, dear God," Mandie added. "Please make President McKinley well. Thank you."

"Please, answer our prayer," Celia said.

"Amen," Aunt Phoebe said. She held the two girls back and looked into their faces. "Now we done all we kin do. We hafta trust de doin's of de Lawd.''

Mandie wiped her tears with the sleeve of her nightgown and sat up.

"Thank you, Aunt Phoebe," Mandie said as the old woman got to her feet. "And, Aunt Phoebe, please let me know if you hear anything at all about President McKinley . . . please."

The old woman walked toward the door. "I'll do dat, Missy," she said as she opened the door. "Now I has to go. Dat bell gwine ring any minute now fo' you girls."

"Thanks, Aunt Phoebe," Celia said.

Aunt Phoebe walked into the hallway just as Mandie remembered something else. She ran to her side and said, "I'm sorry I forgot to thank you for taking Snowball during our tea party this afternoon. I ruined my white gloves, but I didn't soil my dress, thank goodness. If you hadn't come along and taken him, I don't know what I would have done. He would have ruined my dress."

The old woman smiled and said, "Dat smart cat. I keeps tellin' folks dey jes' don't know how smart dat cat is. He wanted outta my house real bad. He tried de doors, de windows, and den he decided on de fireplace. I was in de kitchen and heerd sumpin' in de parlor, but by de time I gits to de room, I sees him disappearin' up dat chimney."

Mandie smiled and said, "He has done that before—gone up a chimney. Do you think he'll try it again?"

"No, he cain't do dat now," the woman said. "Cal, he done kivered up de fireplace wid some pieces of wood. And pritty soon, we be havin' to have a fire lit to stay warm, so dat'll put a stop to dat."

"It's good the fireplace in our room here has a closer in the chimney, or he'd probably have tried it," Celia remarked.

"My grandmother should be home tomorrow night, according to what Annie told Uncle Cal. I can take Snowball over to stay with her," Mandie said. "I hope she is home by then. There's so much I want to talk to her about."

Aunt Phoebe looked from one girl to the other, frowned, and said, "I be tellin' things I ain't s'posed to know." She softly closed the door and stood inside the room. "But from whut I hears, dem people whut named Halibut, dey wants dis heah school—"

Mandie gasped and interrupted, "You mean they are going to buy it? Oh no, I haven't even been able to talk to my grandmother about it yet. I was hoping they would be slow in making their decision."

"Oh, but, Missy, it ain't a sho' thing," Aunt Phoebe said. "It all 'pends on dat Mistuh Chadwick givin' dat Mistuh Halibut a job, too. But dat lady, she sho' want dis heah school."

Mandie and Celia looked at each other. "We'll probably see Tommy and Robert at church tomorrow, and if we can get a chance to speak to them, we'll ask what they know about it," Mandie said to Celia. "*If* we can get a chance when Miss Prudence is not close enough to hear."

Celia agreed.

"I gwine go now," Aunt Phoebe said, opening the door again.

"Oh, Aunt Phoebe, I know I'm a lot of trouble, but please let me know, just as soon as Uncle Cal finds out, whether my grandmother is home or not," Mandie requested.

"Dat we will," the woman said. "But, Missy, I wouldn't advise you to go runnin' to Grandmama's widdout Miz Prudence sayin' you kin, 'cause you already be in much trouble."

"I know, Aunt Phoebe. I'll remember you told me that," Mandie agreed. "I'll just wait to see what happens."

"Good-night now, girls," the woman said as she walked out into the hallway.

"Good-night," Mandie and Celia replied as Aunt Phoebe closed the door behind her.

"She's right, Mandie," Celia said. The girls sat back down in the chairs. "If she has an agreement with the Halibuts to buy the school, she won't need your grandmother's money now. Therefore, she might not have to be lenient with you."

"I know," Mandie said. "But I still have to talk to my grandmother for several reasons. It seems strange she'd be out looking for Hilda for all this time. Somehow, I'm going to talk to my grandmother when she gets home."

The curfew bell finally rang, and the two girls blew out the lamps and jumped into bed.

Mandie tossed and turned all night. She had bad dreams about President McKinley, her grandmother, and Hilda.

Chapter 10 / Joe Arrives

All the students at the Misses Heathwood's School for Girls were required to attend church on Sunday, and they went to the same one Mrs. Taft attended. After they were dismissed from the breakfast table on Sunday morning, Mandie and Celia rushed upstairs to get dressed.

"I'm in a hurry to get through this day, so I can see my grandmother tonight," Mandie remarked as she slipped on a new blue silk dress that Aunt Lou had made for her.

"I hope she has come home by tonight," Celia said as she took down a lacy dress made of lavender crepe.

"I don't think I've ever been so frustrated in my life," Mandie said as she buttoned the tiny pearl buttons down the waist of her dress. "I feel like I'm running backward and I'm nearly out of breath."

"But you can't change facts," Celia said. She

pulled her dress over her head and shook down the long, heavy skirt.

"I don't know about that. Sometimes you can do things that will influence the outcome of whatever you're trying to do," Mandie said, looking in the mirror. She tossed back her long blond hair and then pulled it up on top of her head. "You know, Celia, I think it's time we wore our hair up and had a proper hat to wear instead of bonnets. After all, we're thirteen years old."

"I like that idea, but we'd have to convince our mothers to buy the hats, and I have an idea that would be impossible," Celia replied as she tied the ribbon sash on her dress.

"I don't know," said Mandie. "I think I'll discuss it with my grandmother." She brushed out her hair, then, with a smile, looked at Celia and said, "Besides, how are we ever going to get boyfriends while we're wearing bonnets?"

Celia looked shocked and replied, "Oh, Mandie, you know we're not old enough to keep company with boys. Whatever made you say that?"

Mandie shrugged and said, "Some girls are married at sixteen years old, Celia. I don't plan on getting married young, because I have so much I want to do in my life. But I don't want to keep looking like my mama's baby girl, either." She frowned as she pinned back her hair with hairpins and left it hanging loose.

"Mandie, don't rush things," Celia said, joining her before the mirror.

"Celia, I have an idea," Mandie said with a big grin. "Why don't we go to the clothing store downtown one day and just buy ourselves hats? We have enough money." She watched Celia for her reaction.

Celia whirled around to face her. "If we bought hats, what would we do with them?" she asked.

"The older girls here at the school wear hats, and they're probably fifteen or sixteen years old," Mandie said. She straightened up and added, "And we look just as old as they do."

"Oh, Mandie, we'd better hurry and get downstairs if we're going to get seats together in the surrey going to church," Celia said.

The school owned a fancy surrey that was used on special occasions, such as going to church. Uncle Cal had it waiting at the front door when Mandie and Celia came downstairs. The other students were already sitting in the parlor.

The two girls stepped out onto the front porch to speak to the old man.

"Good morning, Uncle Cal," Mandie greeted him as he sat on the steps. "Are the Halibuts going to church with us?"

"No, Missy, dem people done left early dis mawnin' in dey own carriage," he told her.

"Did they go to Mr. Chadwick's school?" Mandie asked.

"No, I hears dem tell Miz Prudence dey go straight home," he said.

Mandie looked at Celia and said, "Then they had probably already been to Mr. Chadwick's school to talk to him."

"They must have gone over there before they came here," Celia said.

"And the boys were probably in class and just didn't see them," Mandie surmised.

Miss Prudence came out onto the porch and the other girls followed.

"All right, young ladies, let's go," the woman said, leading the way to the surrey.

At the church, the girls sat in the section of pews reserved for them. Mandie looked across the aisle and saw Mr. Chadwick's boys in their seats. She smiled at Tommy as he caught her eye.

The service, devoted mostly to the plight of President McKinley, was extra long that day.

"The latest news is that our beloved President is holding his own," the pastor told his audience. "Maybe that's because so many people have been praying for him. But we must continue to remember him in our prayers."

Mandie felt a ray of hope upon hearing this message. She wished she could visit the President personally and encourage him to fight the battle for his life. The very thought of what had happened to the good man sent a pain through her heart. When her grandmother came home, she would have some-one else who knew him to talk to. It was too much to hope that Uncle Ned would visit her before the end of the next week, as he had planned.

Mandie got lost in her own thoughts until the service ended and everyone rose to leave the church. She glanced at Tommy and slipped to the end of the pew to whisper something to him as he filed out with his classmates.

"The Halibuts are gone, and I think they've already been to see Mr. Chadwick," she said, just loud enough for Tommy to hear as he paused for a moment by the end of her pew.

"We know that nothing is settled yet," the boy whispered back as the line moved forward.

Mandie took a deep breath and said to herself, "Thank goodness!"

The girls followed Miss Prudence toward the front door.

As she reached the front door, Mandie almost bumped into Joe Woodard, who was waiting for her there. "Oh, Joe, I'm so glad to see you," Mandie said in surprise.

"I saw you and waited here to catch you," Joe explained.

Miss Prudence looked back. She stopped to watch and said loudly, "Amanda, please stay in line."

Mandie quickly asked, "Miss Prudence, please allow me to speak to Joe for a minute about my grandmother. Please."

"All right, but only one minute. Then you must join us to go back to the school. Now hurry." The headmistress once again continued walking out the door with the other girls.

Mandie stepped out of the way of the other people leaving and said to Joe, "When did you get here? Are you staying at my grandmother's?"

"My father and I arrived early this morning, but your grandmother is still not home," Joe told her. "Annie insisted that we stay there, that Mrs. Taft had left word for us to use her house whenever we got into Asheville."

"Annie said she's expected back tonight," Mandie told him. "Oh, Joe, you just can't imagine what all has been going on since I came back to school."

"I can imagine, all right," Joe said with a big smile. "But do you know that Hilda ran away, according to Annie, and your grandmother has been searching everywhere for her?"

"Yes, that's what Annie told me," Mandie said. Glancing out the open door, she saw Miss Prudence motioning for her to come to the surrey. "I have to go now, but I'll be over to my grandmother's after supper tonight. And I'll tell you what else is happening. See you then."

"All right. I'll be waiting," Joe said with a big smile as Mandie looked back at him and then joined the line of girls getting into the surrey.

When the girls returned to the school, they hurried to leave their bonnets, gloves, and Bibles in their rooms before they got in line for the noon meal. Polly Cornwallis was ahead of Mandie and Celia as they waited to get into the dining room, but when she saw them, she gave up her place to move back and talk to them.

"I saw you talking to Joe at church, Mandie," Polly said. "Is he staying at your grandmother's house?"

"Yes, he and his father are at my grandmother's house, Polly," Mandie told her. "And I don't know how long they're staying."

"Is he coming over to the school while he's in Asheville?" Polly asked.

"I don't think so," Mandie said. "I'll see him when I go over to my grandmother's."

"You will? When?" Polly asked.

"I don't know yet. I have to ask Miss Prudence first," Mandie replied.

The line started to move toward the dining room door. Polly turned and followed the other girls, and Mandie gave a sigh of relief. The last person she wanted to discuss her plans with was Polly. She knew Polly couldn't always keep a secret.

As Celia and Mandie walked along, Polly looked at Mandie again and asked, "Do you think I might be able to go with you to your grandmother's?"

Mandie groaned inwardly. "I doubt it, Polly," she told the girl. "The school has rules about going off to visit, and I will have to get special permission."

Polly gave her a doubtful look as they passed through the doorway and into the dining room, where all conversation had to cease.

As soon as the meal was over, Mandie waited outside the doorway for Miss Prudence to come out. Finally, the last student left the dining room, and the schoolmistress was right behind her.

"Miss Prudence, could I please see you for a minute?" Mandie asked as she stepped up beside the woman.

Miss Prudence hesitated, looked closely at Mandie and then said, "Why, of course, Amanda. Let's just walk on down to my office."

Once they were in the office, Miss Prudence motioned Mandie to a chair. The woman sat down behind her desk and then asked, "Well, what is it you want to talk about, Amanda?"

"Miss Prudence, my grandmother is supposed to return home tonight, and I was wondering if you would allow me to go over to her house for a few minutes," Mandie said quickly. "You see, I could take Snowball, too."

Miss Prudence looked at Mandie and asked, "And what time is it that she'll be getting home?"

"I don't know yet, but Annie, the maid, said she would be home tonight," Mandie said. "I would imagine it would be around suppertime, because I know my grandmother doesn't like to travel after dark."

"Well, in that case, I suppose you may ask Uncle Cal to take you over," Miss Prudence agreed.

"Oh, thank you, Miss Prudence," Mandie said with a big smile. "I'll ask Uncle Cal."

"Now mind you, Uncle Cal will have to wait there and bring you back," the schoolmistress said. "Therefore, you will only be able to stay a few minutes."

"Yes, ma'am," Mandie said. "I understand. Thank you."

"You may go now," the schoolmistress said.

"Yes, ma'am," Mandie said, hurrying out the door and down the hallway to find Celia.

Thank goodness she didn't mention the trouble Snowball caused at the tea yesterday, Mandie thought. *Miss Prudence must not have a definite answer from the Halibuts yet. Therefore, she still wants my grandmother's money, so she has to be lenient with me.*

Mandie found Celia on the front porch, and together they went looking for Uncle Cal. They found him sitting on the front porch of his house in the backyard.

The girls sat down on his steps and Mandie asked, "Guess what, Uncle Cal? Miss Prudence gave permission for you to take me to my grandmother's tonight, and she told me you would have to wait to bring me back."

"Dat be fine, Missy, but yo' grandmama, she ain't home yit," the old man said.

"Would it be possible for you to check later today, to see whether she has returned or not?" Mandie asked.

"I sho' will, Missy," he said. "And I'll let you know."

"Thank you, Uncle Cal," Mandie said as she stood up. "Do you think I could get Snowball and take him for a walk around the yard on his leash?"

"You sho' kin, Missy," the old man said. Uncle Cal left his chair and went through the front door to fetch the cat.

"Mandie, are you sure you won't get in trouble with Snowball?" Celia asked.

"Don't worry. I'll hold on to his leash, and he won't be able to get away," Mandie assured her.

When the old man came back outside with Snowball walking at the end of his leash, the cat saw his mistress and immediately went to rub around her ankles.

Mandie stopped to talk to him. "Snowball, I do love you," she said. "It's just that things are—well, unsettled right now. I'm going to take you to Grandmother's house soon. You'll have that great big house to roam around in."

Snowball looked at his mistress, meowed loudly, and then rubbed his head against her hand. Mandie laughed and said to her friends, "You'd think he understood what I was saying."

"He probably do," Uncle Cal said. "Cats is smarter than people thinks."

Mandie, afraid Miss Prudence would see her in the backyard, had second thoughts about walking the cat, so she gave Snowball back to Uncle Cal. She and Celia walked around to the front porch. The place was deserted—evidently the other girls were inside the house.

"Let's sit in the yard," Celia suggested as she led the way to a bench under one of the huge magnolia trees.

Mandie joined her, and they talked about nothing much for what seemed hours before they finally decided to go to their room.

Time passed, and finally it was suppertime. Mandie had not seen or heard from Uncle Cal. She assumed her grandmother was probably not back yet.

After the evening meal, Mandie was really getting nervous. *Where is Uncle Cal? Why isn't Grandmother home?* she worried. She and Celia went outside and sat on the front porch to wait for Uncle Cal. As the sun was setting, she saw the old man coming up the driveway in the rig.

Mandie hurried to meet him. "Is my grandmother home yet?" she asked eagerly.

"She sho' ain't yit, Missy," the old man said as he threw the reins over the hitching post and took a box from the rig. "Had to git mo' books from dat Mistuh Chadwick fo' Miz Prudence. Gotta take dem into de office." He started walking toward the front door.

"Are you going back to my grandmother's later?" Mandie asked as she followed him.

"I don't 'spect so, Missy. It be gittin' dark, and we soon be hearin' dat bell ring fo' you young ladies to go to bed," Uncle Cal said as he went on through the front door.

Mandie turned back to Celia on the porch and gave her a questioning look. "Oh, what will I do?" she said with a big sigh.

"I'd say there is nothing you can do. You'll just have to wait until tomorrow," Celia said as they sat down in rocking chairs.

"I thought surely my grandmother would be home before dark," Mandie said. "And I suppose by this time, Joe knows I'm not coming over there."

"Let's go to our room and get comfortable, Mandie, before that bell rings for curfew," Celia suggested.

"Guess we might as well," Mandie agreed.

When they got to their room Celia started to undress, but Mandie said, "Wait, Celia. Don't undress yet, I have an idea."

"Oh, Mandie, evidently not a *good* idea," Celia said. Leaving her sash tied, Celia looked at her friend.

"Sit down a minute," Mandie said as she plopped into one of the big chairs.

Celia sat in the other one. "Well?" she asked.

"As soon as the curfew bell rings, I'm going to slip out and go over to my grandmother's house," Mandie said.

"Mandie!" Celia exclaimed.

"And you are going to have to let me back into the house, because all the doors will be locked by the time I get back," Mandie said.

"But, Mandie, how will I know when to open the door?" Celia asked. "I won't know when you get back."

"All you have to do is watch out the window here. I'll come through the yard right down below where you can see me," Mandie explained. "Then you can run down and open the back door to let me in."

"Mandie, that is risky. Suppose someone sees you through another window," Celia said. "Or suppose I run into someone in the house."

"Everyone is supposed to be in their room with the lights out when that bell rings, remember?" Mandie said.

"How long will you be gone?" Celia asked.

"Suppose I go to sleep watching for you. Then what?"

"Oh, Celia, I know you well enough to know you aren't going to sleep until I get back," Mandie said with a little laugh. "And I won't be gone long. I promise."

"I don't think you ought to do this, but if you insist, I suppose I'll have to do what you ask," Celia finally agreed.

"Thanks," Mandie said. She got up and went to the chifferobe. "I'm going to wear my navy blue cape over this light-colored dress. That way I won't be so visible in the dark." She pulled the garment down from a hanger.

The bell began ringing, and Mandie said, "Now I'll wait just a few minutes. Then I'll slip down the back stairs and out the back door."

"Please be careful," Celia cautioned her.

Mandie put on the cape and pulled the hood over her blond head. "You can watch out the window if you want to make sure I get out, and please don't forget to watch for me to come back and run down and let me in."

Mandie walked across the room and softly opened the door. As she slipped into the hallway, she waved back at Celia, then hurried to the back staircase. The steps were dark, but she knew the way because she had been up and down them many times. She also knew how to unbolt the back door.

Mandie found the shrubbery that grew below her window, stepped back from the house, and waved to Celia upstairs. Then she rushed down the driveway to the road. It wasn't very far to her grandmother's house.

Chapter 11 / Nighttime Visit

Mandie practically ran all the way to her grandmother's, and when she finally made it to the front door, she was all out of breath. She quickly knocked and then stood back, trying to slow her breath and calm her racing heart.

When Annie opened the door and found Mandie standing there, she gasped in surprise. "Lawsy mercy, Missy, whut you doin' heah dis time o' de night?" She stepped back to allow Mandie to enter the hallway.

"Is Grandmother home yet?" Mandie managed to ask between quick breaths.

"She sho' ain't yit," Annie told her.

"Then I'll just wait a while to see if she comes home," Mandie said. "Where are Joe and Dr. Woodard?" She removed her cape and hung it on the hall tree.

"In de pahloh, Missy," Annie said.

Mandie hurried down the hallway to the parlor.

As she entered the doorway, she found Joe and Dr. Woodard reading. They looked up and rose to greet her.

"Well, I see you finally made it," Joe said.

"How are you, Miss Amanda?" Dr. Woodard asked.

"I'm fine, Dr. Woodard, and I hope you are, too," Mandie said with a smile. "Annie says my grandmother is not home yet." She walked over to sit down in a chair near Joe.

"Not yet, but any minute, we hope," Dr. Woodard said.

"How did you get here?" Joe asked as he sat down.

Mandie looked at him and smiled. She shrugged and said, "I walked."

"Miss Prudence allowed you to walk all the way here by yourself?" Dr. Woodard asked.

"It's really complicated, Dr. Woodard," Mandie began. "You see, I asked permission from Miss Prudence to visit my grandmother, and she granted it, and told me to ask Uncle Cal to drive me over here and back. But not long ago, Uncle Cal came back to the school and said my grandmother was not home, that it would be too late for me to come over here tonight, anyway." She paused.

"So you just took off all by yourself," Joe said, frowning.

"It's important that I see my grandmother as soon as possible," Mandie said.

"But, Miss Amanda," Dr. Woodard asked, "suppose you are caught disobeying school rules?"

"With all the trouble I've been innocently accused of lately, I suppose it's worth the risk, because it is so important that I talk with my grandmother," Mandie insisted, straightening her long skirt.

Joe stared at her, and Dr. Woodard scratched his head as he looked away.

Mandie couldn't stand the silence, so she tried to explain. "You see, someone has been doing things, and I'm getting blamed. But nobody believes me when I deny doing them. Then along come these people named Halibut, who are interested in buying our school, and I've just got to see my grandmother to convince her to stop them."

"Your grandmother? How can she stop these people from buying your school?" Joe asked. "Your grandmother can't control everybody and everything, Mandie."

"I know that, but she does have enough money to buy the school if she wants to," Mandie explained.

"Do you think your grandmother would want to take on that kind of responsibility?" Dr. Woodard asked. He smiled and said, "I don't think I'd want to have to keep up with all you young ladies."

"I don't know if she needs to actually buy it. She could even give a big enough donation to Miss Prudence and Miss Hope to keep the school running until I at least finish," Mandie said. "I understand they need money to keep the school open."

"Well yes, your grandmother might want to do such a thing," Dr. Woodard agreed, thoughtfully.

Mandie heard a door open and close. "You say Amanda is here?" came her grandmother's voice, loud and clear.

"Yessum, in de pahloh," Mandie heard Annie reply.

Mandie jumped up and was about to rush to

meet her grandmother, but she suddenly became worried about being there without permission. *What would her grandmother say?* she wondered.

Mrs. Taft appeared in the doorway and came into the room. "Amanda, dear, are you here for the night?" she asked as she approached Mandie and the others.

Mandie didn't want to explain, but as she tried to figure out what to say, her grandmother went on.

"Dr. Woodard and Joe, I received your message saying you would be coming to Asheville, and I'm so glad you decided to stay with us." She sat down with a sigh of relief.

"Yes, ma'am, thank you for asking us," Dr. Woodard replied. "I trust you had a fruitful journey."

"Yes, thank you, Mrs. Taft," Joe added.

"No, we haven't been able to find Hilda yet," Mrs. Taft explained. "I've had Ben driving me all over the countryside to every house that we've ever taken Hilda, but no one has seen her."

"Grandmother, what, happened? Did Hilda just disappear one day?" Mandie asked.

"We went to visit the Adamses last Saturday. You know them, Amanda, they live down Tunnel Road," Mrs. Taft explained. "They have a little daughter that Hilda seems to like, and since Hilda can only speak a few words, the little girl loves to get her own books out and read to Hilda. We adults left them together in their back parlor while we had tea. And when it was time for us to return home, Hilda was nowhere to be found."

"Did the little girl not know where she went?" Dr. Woodard asked.

"No, all she could say was that Hilda went out the back door," Mrs. Taft explained. "We couldn't find her anywhere. We searched the whole house and all over the grounds."

"I hope no harm has befallen her," Dr. Woodard said. "Even though she is almost as big as Miss Amanda, her mind isn't developed and she could get in trouble."

"I don't understand why she would just walk out of their house like that," Mrs. Taft said. "We've all done our best to make Hilda realize that we love her, and that this is her home. But I suppose she doesn't understand that."

Mandie suddenly looked up and saw Uncle Ned standing in the doorway. She ran to him, saying, "Oh, Uncle Ned, I'm so glad you're here."

"I come and help Grandmother find Hilda," he said.

Mandie grabbed his old, wrinkled hand in her small, soft one. "I wanted to talk to you about President McKinley. It's all so horrible that I can't believe it." Her voice trembled.

Uncle Ned led her over to the sofa, where they sat down. "Papoose must trust Big God," he said.

"I know, but I wish I could be with the President and tell him I love him," Mandie said sadly. "And his wife must be worried sick."

"Amanda, I sent a telegram expressing our love and best wishes for recovery to President McKinley as soon as I heard the news," Mrs. Taft said. "If he is able to receive his messages, then he knows we are thinking about him."

"And I wrote him a note, too," Joe said.

"My granddaughter, Sallie, wrote, too, for all Cherokee people," Uncle Ned said.

Mandie felt left out. She had not even thought to write the President a note. "I heard that he was shot twice, and was unable to talk to people, according to the newspaper story Miss Prudence read to us," she said.

Mrs. Taft suddenly looked directly at Mandie and asked, "Amanda, are you spending the night here, dear?"

"No, Grandmother, I have to go back to school, but I need to discuss something with you that's urgent," Mandie said, glancing around the room at the others.

"It's late, Amanda," Mrs. Taft said. "Is this matter important enough to keep you out of school past curfew?"

"Yes, it is, Grandmother," Mandie answered. "If we could just talk for a few minutes, I can explain. Then I'll go back to the school."

Mrs. Taft looked puzzled as she rose and said, "All right." She looked at the others and said, "If the rest of you all will excuse us, I'll talk with Amanda in the back parlor so she can get back to school."

Mandie followed her grandmother to the other parlor, where they sat down on a small settee.

"Well, Amanda?" the woman asked.

"Oh, Grandmother, Miss Prudence has had these people named Halibut in to look us over and see if they want to buy the school, and nobody wants them to get it. Will you please, please buy the school to keep those people from getting it?" Mandie asked, all in one breath.

Mrs. Taft looked at her in surprise. "Buy your school?" she asked. "Why, Amanda, what do I want with a girls' school?"

Mandie put on her best smile and said, "Because your only granddaughter happens to be a student there."

"That's not good enough reason for me to get involved with your school," Mrs. Taft objected.

"But, Grandmother, if those people buy my school, I think I wouldn't want to go there any longer," Mandie said. "You just ought to meet these people. They are not friendly and look so stern. They came Friday night and didn't leave until this morning. And Miss Prudence had the boys from Mr. Chadwick's school over for a tea to show the Halibuts what the students are like."

"Amanda, I am too tied up right now trying to find Hilda to get involved in anything else," Mrs. Taft said. "So if these people do buy the school, and if you are not satisfied, then we'll find you another school."

"Grandmother, I overheard Miss Prudence and Miss Hope talking, and they were saying they needed a large donation to keep the school in business," Mandie said. "Maybe you could just give them enough money so they wouldn't have to sell the school."

"I didn't realize they were in such desperate need," Miss Taft said. "Are you sure that is what they were talking about?"

"Yes, ma'am," Mandie said, looking up at her grandmother. "I'm positive."

"Maybe that's why they suddenly decided to retire. That would be the easy way to get out of that position. No one would ever know they were in financial difficulty," Mrs. Taft surmised. "And they are proud ladies."

"You're probably right. So, you see, if you just helped them out, maybe they wouldn't sell the school," Mandie said with a big smile.

"I'll go speak to them the first thing tomorrow. But now, tell me, Amanda, are you away without permission tonight?" Mrs. Taft asked sternly.

Mandie dropped her eyes and said meekly, "Yes, Grandmother, I am. But I was so concerned over President McKinley and over the school maybe being sold, I had to talk to you."

Mrs. Taft stood up and said, "All right, young lady, you will go back to school immediately. I'll ask Uncle Ned to take you."

They went to the parlor, and Uncle Ned agreed to drive Mandie back to the school. Joe asked to go along, and he volunteered to help Ben, Mrs. Taft's driver, get the rig ready. Uncle Ned had come on horseback and did not have a way of taking Mandie back without using Mrs. Taft's rig.

Mrs. Taft went to the door with Mandie when she left. Uncle Ned and Joe were waiting in the rig outside.

"Grandmother, you will come to talk to Miss Prudence tomorrow, won't you?" Mandie asked as they stood at the door.

"I said I would," Mrs. Taft told her. "Now you had better just hope no one sees you going back to the school."

"Yes, ma'am," Mandie said. She was about to leave, but she remembered something very important and turned back to say, "Oh, Grandmother, Snowball is staying with Aunt Phoebe and Uncle Cal. I brought him with me from home and was planning to bring him over to stay with you, but—"

"Amanda, don't worry, I will keep him for you. I'll pick him up when I go to see Miss Prudence tomorrow. Now hurry," Mrs. Taft assured her.

Mandie started out the door, then once again turned back to speak to her grandmother. "I would appreciate it, Grandmother, if you would keep me up to date on news about President McKinley. There is only one newspaper at the school, and it's hard to get hold of it."

"Yes, dear," Mrs. Taft said. "After I discuss these matters with Miss Prudence, I must continue my search for Hilda, but I'll see that you are informed. Good-night."

"Good-night, Grandmother," Mandie said, walking out toward the rig. "I love you," she called back, but Mrs. Taft had already gone inside and closed the door.

She stepped up into the rig, and Joe moved over so she could sit between him and Uncle Ned. The old man started the horse down the driveway toward the road.

"How long are y'all staying in Asheville?" Mandie asked her friends.

"My father and I will be leaving tomorrow or the next day," Joe said.

"I look for Hilda next day or two," Uncle Ned told her, "then home."

"I sure hope y'all find her soon," Mandie said, pulling the cape around her. "And I sure hope Grandmother can do something about my school."

She noticed her two friends were not very talkative. This made her uncomfortable, and she wondered if she'd offended them.

"I'm glad I finally got to talk to my grandmother about everything," Mandie said.

There was no response. She looked from Joe to Uncle Ned and asked, "Are y'all mad at me or something?"

Joe quickly answered, "Oh no, it's not that, Mandie."

"Then what is it? Uncle Ned, how about you?" she asked.

The old man looked at her through the darkness and said, "Papoose must learn not disobey rules. Bad."

"That's right," Joe put in. "And you mentioned at church that you were already in trouble."

Mandie said with a gasp, "Miss Prudence had already given me permission to come to see Grandmother."

"But she didn't say you had permission to leave the school after curfew, did she?" Joe asked.

Mandie frowned and said, "No, but she didn't say *exactly* when I was to visit my grandmother either."

"But Papoose know must not break curfew," Uncle Ned reminded her.

"Oh, shucks!" Mandie said with a disgusted sigh. "So y'all want to add to the list of the things I've done wrong. I've been accused for things I didn't do, and nobody believes anything I say, so I decided to just go ahead and leave the school after curfew. I needed to talk to my grandmother, and it was all for the good of the school."

"You sure have funny ideas about rules tonight, Mandie," Joe told her.

"Papoose must think before doing," Uncle Ned said as he guided the rig down the road.

Mandie knew she had broken the curfew rule and she felt bad about it, but she was tired and didn't want to talk about it anymore.

The rig rounded the corner of the street that ran by the school, and Mandie said quickly, "Uncle

Ned, please let me out on the road at the end of the driveway. If you go on up to the door, everyone will hear the rig and look out. Besides, I have to go in through the back door. Celia will be watching to let me in."

Uncle Ned pulled the rig to a halt at the school's driveway. He reached to take her hand in his. "Papoose think before doing," he reminded her. "I see Papoose before I go home to Deep Creek. I want to wait and watch till Papoose gets to schoolhouse."

"Thank you, Uncle Ned," Mandie said with a squeeze to his hand as she jumped down from the rig.

"When your grandmother comes over to the school tomorrow, she will probably know when my father and I will be leaving," Joe said. "I'll try to see you again before we go home. Be good."

Mandie started to walk up the driveway and turned to say, "I love you both," just loud enough for them to hear. Then she hurried on to the school.

When she reached the back corner of the house, Mandie could hear Uncle Ned driving the rig down the street. She stepped back from the shrubbery and waved toward the window of her room. This was the signal to Celia to let her in. Their room was on the third floor, and it was so dark Mandie couldn't tell whether her roommate was watching or not. Mandie hoped she was there, and went on around to the back door.

Softly turning the knob, she pushed on the door, but it wouldn't open. Evidently it was still locked, and Celia had not gotten down there yet. She sat on the steps and waited.

"Oh, where is Celia?" she muttered to herself as she stood up and tried the door again to make certain it would not open. It would not, so she plopped down on the steps again. Maybe Celia didn't see her wave at the window, she thought. Maybe she'd better go back and do it again.

Mandie hurried back around the corner of the house and walked out into yard to look up at her window. She squinted, trying to see in the darkness whether Celia was up there or not. It was impossible to tell. She quickly waved and then hurried back around to the door.

Just as Mandie raised her hand to try the knob, the door opened. She could faintly see Celia standing there in the darkness.

"Sh-h-h-h-h!" Celia softly warned her as she grabbed Mandie's hand to pull her inside. She pushed her against the wall and whispered, "Somebody is on the steps behind me."

Mandie held her breath and listened. She couldn't hear a sound. *What was Celia talking about?* she wondered. Mandie couldn't hear anything.

"I don't hear anybody," Mandie whispered to her friend.

"Maybe they're gone," Celia whispered back.

Mandie cautiously moved forward. She softly put her foot on the first step and tested it to see if it would creak. It didn't. She held her breath and put her foot on the next step. It didn't creak, either. She couldn't see up the staircase in the darkness, but she didn't feel anyone else's presence.

"Let's go," Mandie whispered to her friend as she moved up the steps. She reached back and felt Celia's hand touch hers.

"Be real quiet," Celia cautioned her softly.

"There is *nobody* here," Mandie whispered as

she made her way silently up the steps.

They finally arrived at the third floor. The windows there gave enough light for Mandie to see that the hall was empty. She led the way to their room, pushed open the door, and looked around. She couldn't see anyone in the room, either, so she walked in.

Celia followed and softly closed the door.

"Whew!" Mandie said with a sigh of relief. "What was that all about?"

Celia spoke in low tones, "Mandie, there *was* someone on the stairs when I first started down to let you in. I saw you wave, and when I got to the first landing, I heard a step creak ahead of me."

"Are you sure it wasn't you making the noise?" Mandie asked as she began undressing for bed.

"I'm sure it wasn't," Celia said as she jumped into bed. She had already put on her nightclothes. "And while I was just sitting there by the window, waiting for you to return, I thought I heard something in the hallway. I looked outside, but no one was there."

"Oh well, at least we made it back to our room," Mandie said as she tumbled into bed. "If there was anyone there, they were gone by the time we came up the steps. So we don't have to worry about anyone having seen us. Besides, if any of the girls saw us, she wouldn't dare report us. She'd have to explain what *she* was doing out of her room at that time of the night."

"I don't know, Mandie, but I do know I heard someone when I first started down," Celia said. "I waited, and that's what took me so long to get to the door. "Tell me what happened at your grandmother's house. Was she at home?" asked Celia.

"Not when I first got there, but she came in not long afterward," Mandie replied. "And Uncle Ned has been helping her look for Hilda, so he was there, too. And, of course, you knew Joe and his father are staying there while Dr. Woodard visits some patients here in Asheville."

"Did you ask your grandmother to buy our school?" Celia asked as she propped herself up on one elbow.

"Yes, but—" Mandie began, then she explained to her friend that her grandmother had promised to come and talk to Miss Prudence.

Both girls were tired. Celia fell back on her pillow, and Mandie turned over to her side of the bed and curled up to think about all the week's events.

But she soon fell asleep.

Chapter 12 / The Troublemaker

Mandie was sleeping soundly when something startled her awake. She sat up in bed and rubbed her eyes. "What happened? Did something wake me?" she asked herself. She looked around the room in the early morning light but couldn't see anyone.

"Must have been a dream," she muttered to herself and lay back down on her pillow.

Just as she dozed off again, the bell in the backyard started ringing. It was time to get up and get ready for breakfast. Her eyes felt like they were full of sand, but she knew she'd better not go back to sleep. She swung her legs off the bed and reached back to punch Celia awake.

"Time to get up," she told her friend. Celia opened her eyes and slowly sat up. "Seems like I just went to bed," she said.

"I know," Mandie agreed. "But this school schedule must go on, and we have to go with it.

Besides, my grandmother is coming to see Miss Prudence today."

Mandie climbed out of bed and went over to the big chair where she had been sitting the night before. She picked up her shoes, turned to sit down, and gasped. A pile of papers lay on the seat.

"Oh no!" Mandie exclaimed as she examined the papers. "Celia, look! Files from the office! How did they get here? Somebody is determined to keep me in trouble." She sat down on the arm of the chair.

"But who, Mandie?" Celia asked as she rushed to inspect the papers.

Mandie thought hard for a moment, then said, "I don't know how she could do it, but you remember all the trouble April Snow has caused me since I came to school here. I'm not accusing her, but she's the only one who has shown such dislike for me."

"April Snow?" Celia mulled that over. "I'm not sure, Mandie, but I believe April Snow was in different places when the other things happened, so it couldn't have been her."

Mandie fanned the papers in her hand and said, "Now, what am I going to do with all these? If I take them back to the office, Miss Prudence will catch me sure as anything. If I leave them here in our room, Aunt Phoebe will probably find them."

"Do you suppose maybe someone was lurking in the hallway last night when I thought I heard a noise, and they waited until after we went to bed to put these papers in here? Because they sure weren't here when you and I came back upstairs," Celia said.

"Well, doesn't it have to be that way? But who was it? And why did they do it?" Mandie asked.

"I think we'd better get dressed before we're late for breakfast, which will only make matters worse," Celia said, going to take down a fresh dress from the chifferobe.

Mandie stood up and raised the heavy cushion in the chair, thrust the papers beneath it, and pushed the cushion back down. "There! They should be safe there until we can decide what to do," she said.

The girls were just barely dressed when the bell rang, calling them down to breakfast. Mandie took one last look at the chair, then followed Celia downstairs.

After the morning meal, the girls came back upstairs to get their books for their classes. Mandie quickly checked the chair. The papers were still where she had put them. She looked around the room. Nothing seemed to be disturbed.

"Whoever it was hasn't been back," Mandie said as she picked up her notebook and textbooks.

The girls passed their morning taking notes in classes, and it was soon mealtime. Mandie was beginning to worry that her grandmother wouldn't visit Miss Prudence after all.

"She promised she'd come over here today," Mandie said to Celia as they went up the staircase to leave their books in their room.

"But she didn't say what time of the day, did she, Mandie?" Celia asked as they continued up the stairs to their room on the third floor.

As they reached the top step Mandie heard someone running up the attic stairs, which were near their room. She stopped and looked at Celia, who nodded that she had heard it, too. They threw down their books in the hallway and raced for the stairs.

Mandie looked up just in time to see the bottom of someone's skirt as the attic door closed ahead of her. She ran to push the door open, but it wouldn't budge.

"It's locked!" Mandie exclaimed. "Someone went in there and locked the door. It's probably the culprit who put those papers in our room." She banged on the door. "Open the door!" she called.

Celia looked at Mandie and said, "It couldn't be April Snow. She came upstairs behind us and went to her room on the second floor."

Mandie drew up her lips in exasperation. She wondered what was going on. And where had this person been before Mandie and Celia chased her up the stairs?

"You stay here and watch the door to be sure she doesn't come out. I'm going to check our room to see if anyone has been in there," Mandie told her friend as she turned back down the steps.

"But what will I do if somebody comes out of the attic?" Celia asked anxiously, looking at Mandie.

Mandie sighed and said, "I don't know. Just see who it is and scream like you're dying. I'll run back. I won't be gone but a minute."

Celia backed down a few steps and watched Mandie descend the stairs.

Mandie rushed to their room. She saw no evidence that anyone had been in there, and the papers were still under the cushion of the big chair. She and Celia had evidently surprised the girl before she had a chance to cause more trouble.

When she rejoined Celia on the attic stairs, no one had come out of the attic.

"I wonder if that door is locked by a key or a latch," Mandie said, tiptoeing up the staircase.

"Why, Mandie? What difference would that make? If it's locked, it's locked," Celia said, watching her. "I think we'd better go get Miss Prudence."

"No, Celia. I want to catch whoever this is by myself, because they must be the one causing me all the trouble," Mandie whispered. She quietly went up to the door. She bent to examine the keyhole. There was no key showing in the lock. Therefore, she was sure the door must have a latch holding it on the other side.

Mandie softly went back down to whisper to her friend. "There's no key in the lock, so I think we can force it open if it's just a latch on the other side."

"But how, Mandie? Besides, it will make an awful noise if we do," Celia protested.

Mandie shrugged and said, "That's the only way we can get it open. If we both push on it, it might just break the latch."

Celia looked worried. "Well, if you insist," she said with a big frown.

"Come on," Mandie told her. She tiptoed back up to the door and tried to figure out how to push it. She whispered to Celia, "Let's just both push on it as hard as we can and see what happens."

Mandie held up her hands and motioned to Celia. Together they pushed with all their might, but the door didn't budge.

"Let's kick it," Mandie said.

The girls pulled up their long skirts and kicked. That only made a loud racket. When they stopped, Mandie thought she could hear movement inside the attic. Whoever was in there knew they were trying to get in now.

Mandie was getting angry with the door now, and she began beating, banging, and kicking as hard as she could. She felt it move a fraction of an inch, but it didn't open.

Suddenly someone called from down the stairs, "Hey, what are y'all up to up there?"

Mandie looked down and saw Joe Woodard coming up the steps toward them. She came halfway down to meet him and explained. "Oh, Joe, I'm so thankful you're here. Someone's in the attic with the door locked, and we're trying to force it open, and Celia and I just aren't strong enough to do that, but with you helping, we can do it," Mandie whispered in one long breath.

Joe looked at her and asked, "Someone in the attic with the door locked? How do you know?"

"We saw them go in," Mandie explained. "They ran ahead of us and went inside and locked the door. There's not a key in the keyhole, so there must be a latch holding the door, and that should be easy to break."

Celia looked at Joe and asked, "Joe, how did you happen to show up right now when we needed you?"

Mandie turned to listen to Joe's answer. She hadn't even thought to ask why he was here.

"I was sent to find you girls and bring you back down to Miss Prudence's office," Joe said with a sly smile.

Mandie caught her breath, "To Miss Prudence's office? What have I done now?"

"You are trying to break in that door and destroy school property," he teased.

"Joe, please be serious," Mandie said. "Is my grandmother downstairs with Miss Prudence?"

When Joe smiled, she knew the answer. "And my grandmother wants to see me?" she asked.

"Both ladies do," Joe explained. "And they told me to hurry before the bell sounds for the noon meal."

"I'm not leaving these steps until I find out who is in the attic. Because whoever it is must be the person causing all this trouble that *I've* been accused of," Mandie said as she moved up a step.

"Well, then I guess I'll have to help you girls destroy school property and, believe me, I don't think your grandmother is going to like this," Joe said as he stepped around Mandie and examined the door.

"You see, the keyhole is empty," Mandie told him as he stooped to look.

"But they could have locked the door with a key and then removed it from the lock," Joe said. He shook the door.

"I should have thought of that, but I don't think that's the case, because I did manage to get the door to rattle just a little bit," Mandie said.

"I think we can push this open. When I say *three*, let's all push with everything we've got," Joe told the girls.

Celia stepped up and positioned herself in front of the door with them.

"All right, here we go. Ready?" he asked as he watched Mandie and Celia turning their shoulders toward the door. "One. Two. Three!" he said loudly.

The three hit the door with all their weight. It popped open, and the girls fell into the attic. Joe caught his balance and helped them up off the dusty floor. The three friends looked around the room. Old furniture stood here and there, and an assortment of trunks was piled on one side.

"You watch the door, Celia, to make sure no one goes out," Mandie whispered. "Joe and I will search the room."

Celia moved back to the doorway and watched. Joe led the way around the room, and Mandie followed. There was no sign of anyone anywhere.

"Now, how can that be? I saw someone come in here," Mandie said loudly, stomping her foot in frustration. "There's got to be somebody in this room."

"I'm afraid not," Joe said with a shrug. "You probably heard rats."

"Joe Woodard, rats don't wear skirts. I plainly saw the bottom of a skirt as someone came in here," Mandie said firmly.

"Yes, we did see someone, Joe," Celia added from the doorway.

Joe looked around the room and asked, "Well then, where are they?" as he pointed around the room with a broad sweep of his hand.

As the three followed his hand around the room, Mandie looked up and saw Uncle Ned standing in the doorway. "Grandmother of Papoose say come down to office," he said.

"Uncle Ned!" she said in surprise. "We're looking for someone in this attic." She explained what had happened.

Uncle Ned walked around the room and looked behind everything. "Must be hiding place," he said, and kept searching.

Suddenly, Mandie heard someone sneeze. She looked around. Her friends had also heard it. She walked in the direction she thought it had come from, but no one was there. As she started to turn back the other way, the lid of a huge trunk moved slightly.

"Here!" Mandie cried to her friends as she raced to the trunk. Before she got there, the lid opened, and a head came up into view. She was shocked to see the face.

"Hilda!" Mandie looked at her friends and said, "Oh, why didn't we think to look for Hilda here. This is where we first found her, remember?"

Hilda pushed the lid back and stepped out of the trunk. She was covered with dirt from head to toe, but she grinned happily at Mandie as she walked toward her.

"Love," she said as she held out her arms to Mandie.

Mandie, disregarding the dirt, embraced the girl and said, "I love you too, Hilda. But you've been a bad girl. My grandmother has been worrying about you day and night."

"Love," Hilda said again, and breaking away from Mandie, she went to grasp Uncle Ned's old, wrinkled hand. He put his arm around her and said, "Love, too."

"Let's go," Mandie told everyone. "Just wait until Grandmother sees who we've found." She tried to lead Hilda out of the attic, but Hilda pulled away from her and went back to the trunk. Mandie watched as the girl reached inside and pulled out something.

"Your bag!" Celia said with a loud gasp.

"This is my bag," Mandie told Hilda. "Where did you get it?" She knew the girl probably didn't understand her and, therefore, would not answer. Mandie looked at the valise that Hilda now held tightly in her arms. It was her bag. She could tell because she could see where the molasses seemed to have dried up on it. At least it was no longer dripping.

"What is going on up there?" someone called from below. Mandie looked down and saw Miss Prudence, with Mandie's grandmother right behind her, coming up the attic steps.

Hilda ran to Mrs. Taft and embraced her. She dropped Mandie's bag and a pile of papers fell out. Mandie stooped to pick them up and realized they were more of Miss Prudence's files. She sat back on her heels and looked up at the schoolmistress, who was silently surveying the scene.

"Your papers, Miss Prudence. And this is my bag," Mandie explained. "Now we know who has been doing all these things!"

Miss Prudence cleared her throat and said, "Amanda, you have soiled your clothes. Please go to your room immediately and clean up."

"I'm afraid I have soiled mine, too," Mrs. Taft said as she stood back and looked at several spots of dirt Hilda had transferred to her. "But I suppose it's worth it to get Hilda back."

Mandie got up and walked toward the door. Behind her, Miss Prudence said, "When you are presentable, come to my private quarters. We are all having our noon meal there so we can discuss something of importance. Now please hurry."

Mandie glanced from the schoolmistress to her grandmother, but Mrs. Taft wouldn't look at her. Mandie noticed that Joe was grinning, evidently in on the secret, whatever it was. Uncle Ned smiled at her, too. Celia looked puzzled.

"I'll be there in a minute," Mandie said, and raced down to her bathroom to clean up. Looking into the mirror, she found she wasn't really dirty enough to take time to change her dress. Besides, she was anxious to know what was going on. She dusted her dress off with a clean towel, washed smudges from her face and hands, and ran to join the others in Miss Prudence's quarters.

Miss Prudence and Miss Hope had their own rooms beyond the office. The dining table there was covered with food, and everyone else had already been seated. Miss Prudence motioned Mandie to an empty chair and she sat down. Mandie glanced at Hilda, sitting next to her grandmother, and noticed someone had washed her face and hands and combed her hair.

"This is a very special occasion," Miss Prudence began. "Everyone but you and Celia knows already, but your grandmother has bought the school—"

Mandie interrupted in excitement, "Oh, Grandmother, I love you!"

"Amanda!" her grandmother said.

"I'm sorry, Miss Prudence," Mandie apologized.

"Well, with all the things you've been through since school started, I suppose I can forgive you," Miss Prudence said. "But please let me finish. Your grandmother has agreed to purchase the school building. She will lease it back to Miss Hope and me, and we will continue to own the business part. Her wonderful gesture has saved us from selling the school to the Halibuts."

Mandie was so thrilled, she asked question after question, until her grandmother finally said, "I think you've said enough, Amanda. Now I would like to say a little something. Joe told me your father's house seemed abandoned when he and his father passed it on the way here. He told me you were worried about it. Therefore, I have decided that if you would like, you may go home with Dr. Woodard and Joe for a day or two, and check on this."

Mandie jumped out of her chair and ran to embrace her grandmother. "Oh, Grandmother, I love you so much."

"Amanda, please sit down and eat," Mrs. Taft told her. "I'm only doing this for you to show my appreciation for finding Hilda. As soon as I saw you with her in the attic, I decided I would grant you this favor."

Joe looked at Mandie and grinned as he said, "Things are getting better all the time. President McKinley was able to take a little nourishment, and they say he's on the road to recovery."

"Oh, thank the Lord," Mandie said with a big breath.

After all the dark days she had been through lately, the sun was finally beginning to shine. She was thankful for all that had happened. And she reached to grasp Uncle Ned's hand as she looked up into his deep black eyes.

"I thank the Big God," she said, using his term.

"Yes, Big God do good," the old man said.

Now she was looking forward to visiting her father's grave, and if his house was empty, she'd have a chance to roam around the property.

Oh, how she hoped it would be.

Cooking with Mandie!

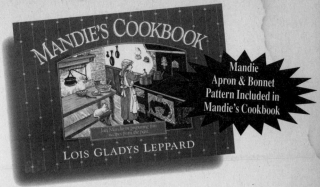

After days and days of begging, Mandie finally convinced Aunt Lou to teach her how to cook. You know who Aunt Lou is—Mandie's Uncle John's housekeeper. Mandie not only loved learning how to cook, but she recorded every recipe, as well as every "do" and "don't" that they went through. And that is how this cookbook came to be.

Mandie also learned how to cook Cherokee-style from Morning Star, Uncle Ned's wife. Sallie, their granddaughter, helped translate, since Morning Star doesn't speak English. Being part Cherokee, Mandie wanted to learn how her kin-people cook.

With Mandie's step-by-step instructions, you can cook and serve meals and share the experiences of girls from the turn-of-the-century. Learn how to bake cakes and pies, do popcorn balls, make biscuits and Southern fried chicken, as well as make Indian recipes such as dried apples and potato skins.

If you love the Mandie Books, you'll love to try cooking Mandie's favorite recipes!